SUNSET SANCTUARY

RJ CASTIGLIONE

RJ CASTIGLIONE BOOKS

SUNSET SANCTUARY

RJ CASTIGLIONE

INTRODUCTION

Sunset Sanctuary touches on a topic that was difficult for me to write, detailing in a very personal way through the use of first-person perspective the thoughts and experiences of the fictional character of Adam Frost, a domestic abuse victim.

While I have never personally experienced domestic violence, I know many who may read this book have. I've taken pains to make sure I portray an honest and gentle experience for the main character wherever possible.

During the midst of writing the first draft, a friend of mine lost her life to domestic violence. Her story has been fictionalized and written into Sunset Sanctuary in remembrance of her (the character of Debbie). Names and details were changed or omitted to respect her family's privacy.

In honor of my friend and with respect toward the subject matter, 10% of the proceeds of all sales of this book for the next year (until March 2021) will be donated to the National Domestic Abuse Hotline:

https://www.thehotline.org/help/

If you or anyone you know is suffering abuse, please know there are people able to listen and help. Go to the website above to chat live with someone, or call their number at **1-800-799-SAFE**. Please find your path to safety. With that said, I hope you enjoy the story.

CONTENTS

1
DAY 1

A FEW OUTFITS, OLD SNEAKERS, MY CELL PHONE, AND A THOUSAND dollars — the contents of my worn satchel the TSA saw as I stood in the airport security line, feet firmly planted on the footprint mat below. I waited for my pat down to end so I could be done with this and get to my gate.

A TSA agent mouthed me a shallow apology after ripping the fabric on my tattered bag, but I didn't care about the satchel enough to mind. It wasn't significant to me. It was my "safety" bag. I joked about it in my head dozens of times when I saw it hidden in the trunk of my car, should I ever gather enough courage to run away. Worse, however, was passing it off as a gym bag when my now ex-boyfriend spotted it. Still, the bag was now split down the middle, held together only by a linen patch with "Adam Frost" sewed on.

I was nervous, sweating, and anxious to get through security and onto the plane before the pain drugs wore off. I picked at the itchy abrasions on my arm, some framed by yellow and purple bruises, doing my best to distract myself from other injuries I tried to hide—a clotted gash on my scalp, a black eye, and some bruised ribs. The fact that I was a mess must have contributed to my being flagged for additional screenings.

The bag-ripper waved me to his table, looking me over once or twice before focusing on the hospital bracelet around my wrist.

"Sir, are you all right?" the man asked.

"Yeah," I said, clenching my jaw in pain as I reached into a pocket, pulling out a slip of paper and handing it to the man, hoping it might speed things along.

The agent's attitude changed as he read the slip, transforming in an instant from passive boredom to a more genuine concern. Through the back of the paper, I could make out the outlines of "Police Report" read in reverse. The slip detailed the events of the last twenty-four hours before I decided to flee the hospital instead of seeing things through to the end.

The man returned the paper, pushed my bag toward me, and waved me into the terminal. I was quick to collect my meager belongings while an obnoxious woman behind me faked a sigh at how slow I moved.

I sat down with my bag and traded my slippers for a pair of ratty sneakers, rounding out my "I look like I have a hangover" ensemble. I winced after pulling my leg up to tighten the laces but gave up before I could reach my foot. With loose sneakers being the least of my troubles, I collected my pack and crept further into the airport at a pace that would make snails bored.

My phone vibrated. I flipped the screen up to find a few dozen missed texts, five new voicemails, and forty missed calls. I answered the current incoming call from Luana Frost, my mother.

"Good Lord, Adam! Where have you been?" my mother asked.

"It's all right, Mom. I just got released from the hospital." My voice cracked against the lie. I didn't want to let her know I checked myself out against the doctor's wishes.

"Just some scrapes and bruises. I'm okay. I'm at the airport." My voice trailed off. My heart skipped a beat as I sensed her concern through the phone, fingers turning white as I clenched the tiny device in my hand. I hated lying to her, especially considering she could always tell.

"Did he—"

"I don't want to talk about it, Mom! I'm losing it here, and I'm getting on a plane. I'm going home." My mother tried to speak again but I didn't let her get a word in. "We discussed this already. Auntie is expecting me. I need to get away from all this. I'm sorry, I don't know when I'll be back."

She sniffled, a sign she was trying her best to choke back her tears.

"I can't do this now, Mom. I'll call you when I get settled."

I hung up the phone before she tried to change my mind. I wasn't going to stay in Atlanta, plus the tickets were already purchased. I was finally escaping. My heart pounded, and I had trouble catching my breath. The buzz of the drugs faded and panic began settling in. A few bruised ribs didn't help any. As the world started to close in on me, I fought against an impending panic attack. Not here. Not now. Nervous energy pulsed through my brain like a faulty power transformer. My hands began to tremble.

Taking a few deep breaths to calm down, I gathered myself and offered my boarding pass to a young woman at the departure gate. She scanned it and motioned for me to board, although she looked worried after noticing my black eye. I took one look back, down the long hallway of Atlanta International Airport, and thought about the city that had been my home for half my life, the city that first nurtured me before beating me to a pulp, and now, spitting me out.

My eyes began to water as I regretted leaving my mother and sister, Maria, behind. They were the only people who knew my full story. They knew why I was running away and from who I was hiding. They wanted me to stay, to face my ex, and to put him in jail, but I had no interest in seeing it through. I certainly didn't want to confront him in a courtroom.

The single thought that dominated my mind was to escape to the island. To get as far away as I could to a place where the last few years couldn't follow me.

I looked at the faces of some young men already seated on the plane. Some of them reminded me of myself five years ago: bright-eyed eighteen-year-olds with tight asses and the whole world at their disposal. They practically twitched at the prospects of love, lust, and alcohol in the years to come.

I leaned patiently against the seat next to me and cracked a tense smile at a young woman with her children blocking my way, reminding me of my mother when she first put us on the plane to Atlanta almost fifteen years before.

As I claimed my own narrow, no-leg-room economy chair, my mood soured even more. Pain jolted through my torso and throbbed in my ears. From the moment the police spotted me unconscious in the street, and the ambulance sped me to the hospital until now, I hadn't a moment to process things. And with my bruised ribs, I indeed didn't have the energy to breathe and relax. A flight attended passed by me.

"Sir, are you okay?" she asked.

I nodded. "Just my back, miss. I threw it out a little." I bit the words out through my clenched teeth.

"I'll take some ibuprofen," I finished as the muscle spasms subsided. Seeing me able to relax in my chair was enough to ease the attendant's concern. She walked away to assist other passengers.

I popped a pill I fished from my pocket and swallowed it dry—a healthy dose of OTC painkillers from the hospital a concerned nurse gave me on my way out. As I flipped through missed calls on my phone, I began to relax more.

"Jeff. Jeff. Jeff. Mom. Jeff. Jeff. Jeff. Jeff. Mom," I muttered to myself. I turned my phone off and put it away, fastened my seatbelt, and closed my eyes to block the sun's glare as it shined through the narrow window next to me.

I brushed my fingers through my black hair and felt a shock as I touched the wound Jeff Thatcher, my ex, gave to me: a dirty ashtray to my head. I reviewed the last few years in Atlanta and how much trouble I'd gotten myself into. How did I fall so deeply in love with a man who treated me like shit? Why did I endure so many beatings? Why did I let him dismantle me so? Why did I still make myself believe that it was my fault? Could it have been avoided?

"Fucking stop," I muttered as the painkiller kicked in. I leaned against the window's cold glass and fell asleep, ready and waiting for my timely return to my childhood home: to the island. To the mountain. To Maui.

* * *

"Sɪʀ?"

I shot upright and winced as my ribs throbbed.

"Sir, we've arrived. You need to disembark now."

I looked around, eyes heavy with sleep. "Where are we? Why hasn't the plane taken off?" The last thing I recalled was shuffling from one gate to the next at LAX for my connecting flight. I looked around me and wondered about the empty plane.

The attendant laughed. "It has. We're here. Welcome to Maui." The young man waved his arms down the aisle of the plane and instructed me again to disembark. My heart skipped a beat as I looked him over from head to toe. He looked a bit too much like Jeff with his broad shoulders, thin nose, and square jaw.

I blinked a few times, still groggy, collected my bag, and left the empty plane. Stepping off the loading bridge, I looked around the airport. It hadn't changed in years: one long hangar with so many windows it felt like I was already outside.

It was late afternoon by the time I made my way out of the airport. I was glad to have no luggage as I pushed my way through the large crowd of tourists waiting for their massive suitcases, golf clubs, and child seats. To any local, I supposed I looked like any other island hopper heading home from Honolulu for the day. Everything felt perfect. Maui was my home, after all. Just like my mother and sister, I was born here. My father was a mainlander and married my mother after being stationed on O'ahu. I went to elementary school here and then left. My dad dragged us to the mainland where nothing made sense—and then left us when he got bored. It took my mom years to admit to herself that it wasn't her fault. The man just didn't want a family.

The air in Atlanta was different. It lacked the sweetness that I knew and loved. On the mainland, where the ocean was nowhere in sight, I often felt I was missing a security blanket. The winters were too cold. The summers were too hot, humid, and absent the gentle trade winds that turned even the warmest day into complete paradise. My father yanked away what I knew and loved and replaced it with a sprawling, urban jungle: a concrete wasteland with too much noise and traffic and people. And folks in Atlanta never felt quite right. They were kind enough, aside from Jeff, but they weren't ohana. They weren't family.

At the curb, I sat down and looked around me. I could see the afternoon clouds pushing their way up to Haleakala's peak to the southeast and the continuous cloud layer over Waikapu. I smiled at a pair of roosters fighting for dominance over a flock of hens only twenty feet away. As expected, the island hadn't changed at all. Even the clouds were the same. Maui was all very comforting, all very predictable.

I slung my pack over my shoulder and walked toward the shuttles, flinching as the strap grazed the wound on my scalp. I was still very much in pain, and the ride to Lahaina was very long this time of day, with all the tourists on their way to the resort strip.

"Howzit, cuz!"

I spun around at the sound of an all-too-familiar voice. I couldn't help but grin. Waiting at the curb, a giant hulk of a man raised his arms to his side to greet me with his broad shoulders, big gut, and a yellow bandana tied around his shaved head.

"Tad!" I said as I hustled as best as I could toward him.

Tad started to wrap me into a bear hug, but I cringed and backed away, afraid of the pain it would cause. He looked concerned. "When Auntie called and told us you was coming, we couldn't believe it. My little cuz back from the mainland." Tad inspected me and saw the bruises on my arms, pain in my eyes, and the egg on my scalp. He grimaced a bit but started leading me away.

"What have they been doing to you over there? You look like a haole!" Tad let out a giant belly laugh.

I knew I was pale and skinny. The mainland made you that way. Hours working in a gaming and comic book store didn't help, either. I realized I was supposed to work again and never called to quit. Given that we broke ten customers on a good day, I knew it wasn't going to be a problem. It wasn't like I was going to make a career out of stocking comic books, laughing at nerd rage, and providing tabletop gamers their chance at a fix. Still, it was a job with people I liked.

"Adam!" Tad gently punched my shoulder. "Where did ya go?"

Tad pulled open the door to his truck. It squealed on its hinges and bobbed up and down as though it would fall off at any moment. It was a rust bucket if I ever saw one. Remnants of blue paint peeked out from behind a thick layer of rust and mud. I recalled all too well the cost of island living: anything metal turned to rust a hundred times faster than anywhere on the mainland. I climbed into the truck as best I could and sank back into the worn passenger seat that felt like it would swallow me whole. Moments later, the engine lurched to life. We sped off to join the line of rental cars driven by dreary-eyed tourists on their way to their condos and hotels.

"Sorry, cuz," I yelled over the noise of the engine. "Just needed to get away from a few things at home. Auntie said she could use my help with the inn. I thought I'd take her up on that offer."

Tad nodded at me. He perked one cheek up into a half-grin. "She sure could. I'm working all day. The house is falling apart. It needs some mad TLC."

I recalled the old estate from my childhood. Despite being on such a small island, it always felt grand. Closing my eyes, I imagined the after-school bike rides to my aunt's two-story colonial home. The building stuck out like a precious gem among an ocean of condos or cottage style homes, although locals often considered it more of an eyesore.

In my mind, it was painted the whitest of white with dozens of windows on all sides. The western windows faced the beach for the most beautiful sunsets behind Lanai. The sunrise over the eastern mountains brought with it a soft fog that amplified the white sand beach. The water was always sapphire blue. And at night, I could be lulled to sleep by the constant sound of ocean waves heard anywhere in the house. I even lived there after my mother and father sold their home before moving to the mainland.

In my heart, however, the house had always called to me. It was heaven, comprised of bottomless pitchers of POG juice, body surfing, and trays full of malasadas, a pastry treat Auntie made her specialty after she learned the recipe from a construction worker who helped her build the house decades before.

It was all so stereotypically Hawaiian. I was not without grand memories of my childhood, island paradise.

My day-dreaming could have gone on for hours, if not for Tad. He stopped the truck halfway to Lahaina as traffic slowed to a crawl.

"Damn haoles! Why they all have to land the same time!" he said, angered by the traffic jam. He punched the radio to turn it on: a low-volume recap of the mainland's greatest hits.

My ears perked up. "You're not upset about just the traffic, are you? There's always traffic."

"About damn time, brah. Thought the plane ride made you mute." He threw a granola bar from his cup holder into my lap, but I set it aside.

"Just pissed. Auntie worked hard on that house. It's her pride and joy; a mainlander's home away from home, ya know? And now the haoles all stay at the massive resorts with all their fancy restaurants, bars, and fake luaus."

Without looking, he pulled the car off the road and into a parking area of some new trailhead I didn't recognize. I looked around and saw some locals working under their rust buckets while chickens ran around looking for their next meal.

Tad seemed more frustrated than the last time we spoke. "Lua," he said as he hauled himself out of the truck and walked up the trail to relieve himself.

I knew things were rough, but I couldn't imagine they were terrible enough to get Tad so worked up. I thought I would be here to do some painting and changing out some furniture. It sounded so much worse. I needed to talk to him now before getting to Lahaina. I turned off the car and pocketed the keys, stepped outside, and leaned against the grill. It was time for some answers.

"Tad, you need to tell me what's going on!" I yelled up the trail. I paused briefly as my ribcage jerked against the force of my yelling. "With Auntie!" I continued with a slight cough.

Tad sauntered back down the trail with a big grin on his face and a freshly fallen coconut in his hands.

"No, Tad. No distractions. Just tell me what's going on."

As he leaned next to me, the car sunk against his weight. "It's not good, brah. You not gonna like it."

I rubbed the back of my neck, kneading out some of the built-up tension I carried from Atlanta. "I'm going to find out anyhow."

"If you really want to know, it started ten years ago. Remember? When she fell. Your mom doesn't know, but she broke her hip. Since then, she hasn't been doing too good. She couldn't afford therapy, so walks kind of stiff-like. She's stuck on the first floor, and that doesn't hold so well for managing the business."

Tad fidgeted with the coconut in his hands, apparently wanting to get back into the car. I gave him the keys, and we climbed back in and took off.

"About five years ago, folks came in and reappraised the property. They hiked up her taxes. She thought about getting an exemption, but word is some mainland firm is eyeing her lot and wants her out. Even though we're doing all we can to make sure she has what she needs, she's barely making ends meet. The more she pays in taxes, the less she has for the property. The less she has for the property, the worse business gets."

I thought about this for a little as traffic in front of us sped up.

"How much does she owe?" I asked.

"Thirty-thousand."

My stomach dropped after hearing the amount. Now almost there, I was glad that I knew what was going on.

"Anything else I should know?"

"Yeah, brah. She still got a bottomless jug of POG in the fridge."

2

EVENING 1

THE DRIVE THROUGH LAHAINA IN THE EARLY EVENING TRIGGERED WAVES OF euphoria. The sights, the smells, and the sunburned tourists all remained unchanged, save a drastic improvement in their fashion sense since the early '90s. There was a lot less neon and armbands. Looking to the east, I saw the dry mountains leading up to Puu Kukui, the lesser of Maui's two long-dormant volcanoes.

One thing had changed, though. I grinned at the sight of two gay men walking hand-in-hand down the sidewalk, dressed in tight swim trunks and muscle shirts. They left little to the imagination.

"See something you like?" Tad joked as he gently punched my arm. I turned away from him to hide my blushing cheeks.

"Just glad to see some of my people here," I said.

"You mean islanders? Or friends of Dorothy?" Tad let out a deep belly laugh. He was as insatiable as I remembered but not unrelenting. And how the hell did he know the term "friends of Dorothy?" He calmed down and turned left onto a small side street only a block from Auntie's house.

My all-too-brief good mood faded when I spotted the house. As we pulled into the parking lot, I saw signs of disrepair everywhere. Tad shifted the truck into park, and we climbed out.

Weeds sprouted out of cracked pavement. The once smooth lot where Tad and I played frisbee and soccer as kids was nothing more than a gravel patch, some areas highlighted in jagged white lines where parking spaces used to be. The white fence surrounding the estate was now a dark gray, faded and cracked from decades of sunlight and salt air.

Slinging my pack over my shoulder, I pressed on until I reached the old picket fence. As I pushed the gate open, some of the wood broke off in my hand, leaving a white powder on my skin that I brushed off on my pants. The house did not fare much better. The front porch's floor creaked under my weight, and the far left side had missing boards that split and fell to the ground below.

The window glass was spotted. Shutters barely hung on their rusted-beyond-repair hinges. The front door was dreary, and the inn's signpost faded and sun bleached. I wiped some of the dirt off the sign and could still see the lettering: "The Estate Inn."

I wondered for a moment how the property passed health and sanitation codes. Maybe Auntie had a friend in the inspector's office. My concerns were pushed aside when I swung the door open and sighed in relief. Although the outside made the entire place look haunted, the inside was clean and tidy, although a bit worse for wear.

I kicked my shoes off and stepped over the worn wooden floors, each step creaking enough to announce my presence to anyone in the house.

"Adam's home!" a cheerful voice boomed from the kitchen. I peeked into the dining room just as Auntie hobbled out of the back of the house. She juggled a tray in her hands with a glass of POG and a malasada on it.

I claimed the tray from her and set it down on the dining table before she pulled me into a firm hug the likes of which I hadn't felt in so long. I melted a bit. Tears welled in my eyes.

"It's so good to see you, Makani!" She kissed my cheek, standing on her toes to reach. My knees buckled a little as relief and emotion washed over me.

"I missed you so much," I choked out, sobbing a little into her blouse. The stress of the last day seemed to strike me all at once. My nose sunk into her cinnamon-scented hair. Hearing Tad thudding into the house behind me, I composed myself and let her go, wiping tears from my eyes before they both became concerned.

"It's good to be back, Auntie," I said as I picked up and downed the glass of juice, an almost too-sweet mixture of passionfruit, orange, and guava, POG for short. I claimed the malasada as well and consumed it in three large bites. I didn't realize how hungry or thirsty I was, having not eaten anything since yesterday.

Auntie took a step closer and pinched my chin in her hand, turning my head from side to side as she examined my black eye. She looked both worried and angry, and I sensed in her a desire to kill my assaulter. I shot her a look that said "I don't want to talk about it."

"Good to see some things haven't changed," I said.

"Bah!" she exclaimed as she released my chin without saying anything about my eye. "If you're referring to my home, you should know as long as there's juice, malasada, and rum, it'll always be the same. But I do have some things for you to do while you're here." Her face lit up as she picked up the now empty tray.

With her free hand, she wiped some sugar from my chin. "Now go to your room, clean up, and get some sleep. It's 1 a.m. to you, and I won't be having you walk around like some drunken zombie tomorrow."

"Zombies don't drink," I joked. She huffed at me and waved me away with her cane.

"You better not disobey your old Auntie Ala," Tad joked under his breath. "She like Madame Pele. You wouldn't wake up in the morning."

He called her by her nickname, Ala, although most folks said her full name, Alana, or called her Mrs. Manalo. Her family and younger friends called her Auntie out of respect.

She smacked Tad on the back of his head. "I'm not that old!" she yelled. "And I certainly don't prey on unsuspecting tourists. Haven't done that in at least a century."

I laughed at the two of them, not only because of their local humor — the idea that Auntie was a vengeful fire goddess — but because they were comfortable in a way only family could be.

Before she scolded me again, I wished them goodnight and made my way up the stairs to my old room. The floorboards creaked with every step I took. I struggled with the shaky railing. At the top level, I peeked around the hallway leading to the guest quarters and grimaced at the sight of a thin layer of dust on the floor. No footprints meant no guests. And no guests meant no money to fix the property.

I scratched the back of my head and twinged when my finger ran across the ashtray-shaped scab hiding under my greasy hair.

"Everything good, cuz?" Tad asked from the bottom of the stairs.

"Yeah. I'm fine."

Tad's voice faded as he yelled his goodbyes to me and left the house. I felt guilty about not asking more about how he was doing. We hadn't talked at length about his life in quite some time, at least not after his father, my uncle, died. I didn't even know what he did for work or where he was staying, although my guess would be the same old shack his dad bought decades ago on the mountain-side of the highway. Most locals couldn't afford homes near the beach. Most didn't even aspire to it, preferring the seclusion residential communities offered from the endless wave of tourists seeking respite in the island's warm waters.

Now awash with exhaustion, I staggered down the opposite hallway to the smaller and more intimate rooms that used to house Auntie and my family. The door to her old apartment was shut and locked, the worn glass doorknob stained from decades of heavy use. I pushed the door a bit, hoping it would spring open and reveal to me memories of Auntie and Uncle from my childhood. I thought about my uncle, her husband, and how I was unable to attend his funeral as a child. My mom couldn't afford the airfare for even herself at the time, just as she couldn't come when her brother died.

I gave up on the door and entered my old room, a tiny corner of the house with two ocean-facing windows, a twin bed, a wardrobe, and a small bathroom.

Warm, moist air overwhelmed me when I entered. The room remained unchanged from the last time I left it. I even saw some of my toys collecting dust in the corner. I sat on the bed and strained down to pick one up — a white plastic truck with a crack on the hood.

I imagined my seven-year-old self throwing a temper tantrum when I couldn't pack it for our flight to the mainland.

"We'll buy you a new one when we arrive," my mother had said, trying to comfort me. That never happened. Even though she forgot, I never did. And when my birthday rolled around that very first year in Atlanta, the only present I got was my father walking out the door. We couldn't afford many toys after that.

I bent down again and slid the truck under my bed. My ribs throbbed as my torso compressed, causing me to collapse on my side, gripping my ribcage as I slowly stretched out again.

It took me a good two minutes of wincing and controlled breathing before the pain subsided. When I opened my eyes, I saw a glass of water on the nightstand with a bottle of ibuprofen next to it. Beads of condensation slid down the glass, forming a ring on the apple-crate table. Tad must have put them there before he came to pick me up. Which meant my mother told Auntie what happened, and Auntie told him.

It took most of my available energy to sit upright and open the bottle. I popped three of the pills into my mouth and swallowed them with a healthy gulp of water and sat there for a few minutes hoping the pills would chase the pain away. They didn't.

I stood up instead and moved to the windows, sliding the painted iron lock on each of them before pulling them open. The rope-glided windows raised with ease. I inspected the cords securing the windows and saw they had been recently replaced, either by Tad or some friend of Auntie's.

"When did she have the time to get this done?" I asked myself. I jumped at the sound of the door slamming shut behind me, closed by the draft I created. The cool ocean breeze tickled my skin. The temperature in the room dropped quickly from what felt like a balmy ninety to a more acceptable seventy-five. Who needed air conditioning when you had nature's equivalent?

The sun was low on the horizon and cast a golden glow across the sea. A flock of tourists planted themselves on the beach, eager to see their first tropical sunset.

Under any other circumstances, I would watch it as well. I hadn't seen an island sunset since I was a child, never finding the time or having the money to return to Maui. I wasn't in the mood, though, and trudged into the bathroom to prepare for bed.

I stunned myself after I looked in the mirror. Sunlight reflected off my black eye and made it appear twice as big. I poked the tender skin around my eye. It gave way to a swollen mass of nasty that managed to get worse since I left Atlanta.

I tried to peel my shirt off, but even raising my hands into the air proved too much for me. I resigned myself to brushing my teeth, relieving myself, and returning to the bedroom to collapse for the evening. As I lay there, the last sliver of the sun sank below the ocean horizon, and the room went dark. The noise of applause from elated tourists echoed in the room. I couldn't blame them for their excitement. Maui was a paradise on earth. At the same time, I wasn't like them at all. Where they came here for a treat, I came here to escape.

I flipped my phone open and turned it on for the first time since Atlanta. The tiny device buzzed to life. After inputting my passcode, it continued to vibrate as new messages and missed calls rushed in. Fifty-seven missed calls from Jeff, three-dozen new text messages from him, and a single call from my mother. Jeff's text messages ranged from coherent apologies to drunken nonsense and from sorrow to apathy to anger to rage.

I quickly silenced the phone when it rang again and moved to toss it on the floor, but saw it was my mother calling again instead of Jeff.

"Hey, Mom," I said as I put the phone on speaker.

"Adam, you said you'd call when you landed. That was hours ago." She sounded both sad and angry, precisely like I felt.

"I know, I'm sorry. I'm just really tired right now. I'm already in bed."

"I know you are, honey, but I just need you to know that we're here for you. You never told me what happened."

"You know what happened. You read the police report."

"Did they arrest him?" she asked.

"I don't know. I left before I could find out," I lied. I didn't want her to know Jeff was definitely not in prison. If he were, he wouldn't be able to call me and text me as often as he had. With my mom on speaker, I opened one of the last text messages he sent me:

I don't know where you are, but I'll find you. This isn't over.

My jaw muscles tightened when I read the message. I recalled that night, our argument about forgetting to do his laundry, the ashtray to my head, the punch to my face, the kick to my ribs, and my inevitable blacking out.

I realized I zoned out on my mom. The phone fell out of my hand and landed on the bed. Muffled sounds of her voice diffused into the soft comforter. I flipped the phone over and interrupted her.

"Mom, I'm falling asleep. I'll call you later." The line went mostly silent, save the sounds of her sniffling.

"All right. Give Ala my best. I love you, Adam."

"I love you too, Mom."

I flipped my phone shut and set it on the nightstand beside me. I heard shuffling coming from downstairs, from the ohana suite where Auntie lived. She clicked on her radio. The staticky sounds of island music floated into my room from our open windows. The muffled sounds mixed with the crashing ocean waves. A cold breeze soothed my skin, and the scent of the island lulled me to sleep.

3

DAY 4

I spent my morning at the front desk while Auntie cooked up a storm in the kitchen for the few guests we did have. Every so often, things went wrong at one of the hotels on Ka'anapali Beach, and locals who worked there directed disgruntled guests to the Estate Inn. Sometimes, the guests turned around after seeing the parking lot. But if they were courageous enough to come inside, Auntie made them feel as if they were home.

"You won't find a more romantic setting anywhere on the island" and "just wait 'til you take your first bites of our complimentary breakfast. You'll never want to stay anywhere else" met the guests who ventured inside.

The scent of roasting Portuguese sausages, the earthy smell of coffee, and the sweet notes of vanilla Auntie used in her pancake mix kept me alert. Our guests must have smelled breakfast as well. They stumbled downstairs, grins painted on their faces, eager to fill their bellies before a day spent on the beach.

Their attitude changed when they noticed me, still sporting a minor black eye that reduced only a little over the last four days. At least my scalp no longer hurt. My ribs also felt better. I no longer felt a sharp jolt every time I moved. Now, they were just tender to touch, due to bruising on my entire right side. Over the counter medicine reduced the pain enough for me to function without restriction.

"Good morning, Mr. and Mrs. Jones," I said. "I hope you enjoyed your first night here. If you take a seat in the dining room, we'll be serving breakfast shortly. Do either of you have any dietary restrictions we should know about?"

Both of them shook their heads. The woman, a stout looking mainlander with bushy, black hair offered me a straight smile, shook her head, and dragged her husband behind her into the dining room.

I looked at their hotel registration record. They traveled from Oregon to get here. Like most folks who visited Hawaii, they lived on the west coast. I chewed on my lip when I looked at the room rate they paid. Auntie offered them a steep discount, charging them only $75 a night to entice them to stay after one of the resort hotels up the street lost their reservation.

"Young man?" Mrs. Jones called to me from the next room. I abandoned my station, having no other work to do, and walked into the room, finding her and her husband and their odd seating arrangement, both occupying far ends of the table as though they were king and queen dining in their own little castle.

Auntie usually sits at the head of the table with her guests, I thought. Yet, who was I to correct them? After costs, their four-day stay with us brought in much-needed revenue.

"Yes? Can I help you?" I asked the woman. Tad walked in from the kitchen carrying a tray stacked with food. Too much food for two people to possibly consume in one sitting. Auntie stumbled in behind him with a carafe half-full of coffee shaking in her old, tired hands.

"My husband and I wanted to take a helicopter tour of the islands today. We were hoping you could arrange it and charge it to our room."

I looked at Tad and Auntie, not sure how to respond. I was no concierge, and our little operation was too small to cater to our guests' every whim.

Tad, more accustomed to these types of requests, responded. "I'm sorry, Mr. and Mrs. Jones. It's tough to get same-day helicopter tours. I can give you the number for a company, though. You can call to schedule later in the week." I was taken aback by Tad's "customer service" voice. It seemed, when he spoke to clients, he put on his best show.

Mrs. Jones pursed her lips, displeased by the answer. She glared at her husband, who looked up at her with fear in his eyes as he bit into a thick Portuguese sausage. He tensed up and swallowed his breakfast.

"What would you recommend instead?" Mr. Jones asked.

"Well, if you're interested in adventure, I got some spots open on my afternoon zipline tour. The cost is $110 each."

Mr. Jones coughed when Tad said the price, shocked at the amount. "Is there a discount since we're your guests?"

"Unfortunately not," Tad said. "The zipline company doesn't offer discounts to hotels."

"So you work at this inn and for a zipline company? Interesting," Mrs. Jones said.

The woman sounded snooty, as though Tad having two jobs made him suddenly worthless to her.

Auntie strained as she sat down at the table, sighing as she took weight off her bad hip. I chuckled under my breath after spotting some curlers still locked in her fuzzy, graying hair. She poured herself a cup of coffee from one of the spare place settings. "My nephew doesn't work here," she said. "He's just here for the food."

Mr. Jones laughed. "Our children are the same. They only show up when they want to empty our fridge."

His wife cleared her throat. The room became tense and quiet. Even the trade winds blowing through the house seemed to cease, making the dining room feel stifling.

"I'm sorry, young man. We're going to have to pass on ziplining. I just had my knee replaced," Mr. Jones said. "I think I'll just take my wife to the Whaler's village I read about. We'll do some shopping."

Tad, disappointed they didn't want to go ziplining, walked back into the kitchen. Mrs. Jones perked up. Now that I sat next to Auntie to start on my breakfast, I could see both of them at the same time. The wife's eyes darted about, obviously thinking about all the trinkets or clothing she could buy later in the day. Her husband fumed over his plate, possibly afraid of forking over hundreds of dollars for his wife's shopping dreams.

Tad came back out carrying even more food — a tray of malasadas, and a pitcher of POG juice. Mr. Jones' eyes lit up when he saw the pastry tray. He plucked a malasada off and started downing it even before Tad set the tray down.

Auntie started laughing, pleased he seemed to enjoy his breakfast so much. While she clutched her warm cup of coffee in both hands and blew on it to cool it down, she winked at me. She always seemed to come to life when entertaining and feeding others. Being a proper host was her reason for living. It was the primary motivation behind our fight to keep her little inn alive and operational.

After breakfast, our guests fussed around the inn for a while before they left. Mrs. Jones stumbled in the parking lot as her heels got caught in the broken pavement, and Mr. Jones sauntered behind her, wearing a tacky Hawaiian shirt that contrasted with his sunblock saturated skin.

Tad and I cleared the table while Auntie rested in her favorite chair in the dining room, a perfect place for her since it offered a view of both the beach and the parking lot. There, she could nap or read or talk on the phone while she enjoyed the ocean and kept an eye out for arriving guests. I sat in a chair opposite her with the ocean view to my back. All I could see through the large windows was the decrepit parking lot.

"Sorry, Auntie," Tad said as he packed lunch in his bag. "I can't stay. I got a tour in thirty minutes." He didn't wait for her to respond, but left the inn and jogged out to his truck. As he tore open the gate on the picket fence, a hinge broke. The gate hung half crooked, about ready to fall off. I watched through the window a frustrated Tad rip the gate off and toss it aside. The rest of the sad fence shifted as he pulled the gate off and now leaned to one side, ready to collapse at any moment.

While Tad peeled out of the parking lot, his truck kicking up dust and rock, Auntie shook her head.

"That bumbling oaf broke my gate," she said. She pulled a flask out from a hidden pocket on her apron and swigged the liquor within.

"The fence was already broken, Auntie. It's older than you are."

"Nonsense," she said, taking another sip. "It's brand new."

"Are you kidding me? I helped you build that fence when I was a kid." I snickered at her and watched as she nurtured her flask. "Should you be drinking this early? Should you be drinking at all? Aren't you taking some heavy-duty meds?"

She scoffed at me. "I've been drinking this swill my whole life. It hasn't killed me yet, so why stop now?"

She chuckled and handed me the flask. Sunlight streamed in from outside and reflected off her already rosy cheeks. I took a sip from the flask. The sweet liquor hit my tongue and filled me with warmth. But when I swallowed, I nearly choked. It felt like my throat was on fire. I coughed into my arm and handed the flask back to her.

"What is that? It's harsh!"

"Maui Rum. A friend buys it for me."

I coughed more. The burning moved down my esophagus and lingered in the center of my chest. "A friend, huh? Are you sure he's not an enemy? It tastes disgusting!"

"Then why'd you drink it?"

"Because you handed it to me!"

She smiled and took another sip of her flask before tucking it back into her apron.

"Do me a favor, Makani? Don't tell Tad or your mother about this." She tapped the hidden flask. "It'll be our little secret. I don't want to argue with them."

It took me a second to remember why she called me Makani. When I was a child, Auntie and Mom told me that it would have been my name if my father didn't insist on a western one. Despite and to spite my father, Auntie often called me by that name to this day.

"Your secret's safe with me," I said as I walked across the room and poured a glass of juice to wash down the rum.

"Good, now be a dear and take that dreadful fence down for me?" She eyed the phone next to her. It seemed she just wanted to get me out of the house so she could have time to herself for her daily ritual of calling all her friends scattered over the island to talk their ears off. I never quite understood how people did this. What could they possibly have to talk about for hours and hours every day? My mother was the same way, always on with one girlfriend or another with her long-corded phone stretched all over the house while she cleaned, cooked, or watched TV.

I detested the idea of taking down the fence. Manual labor was so not my style. But I was here to help Auntie, and if she wanted me to take down a fence, I was going to take down a damn fence, even if it wrapped around the entire house and would take me hours to finish. I nodded and stood up, holding my stomach still full from a much-too-large breakfast.

"Great!" Auntie said as she picked up the rotary phone and started dialing numbers. "There are gloves on the porch. Watch out for spiders!"

I found the gloves like she said, sitting under a hammer, ready for me to get to work.

She planned this. Even if Tad didn't break the fence, she prepared for me to take it down today. I shook my head and smiled. Auntie had a way with people. She was good at getting folks to do just what she wanted, although that didn't help her pay her property taxes.

I spent the rest of the morning ripping down the fence. None of the planks could be salvaged. What didn't split apart in my hands was dried and cracked. I used the hammer to bend or remove the nails, placing the rusty spikes in a bucket I found on the porch so no one would step on them. Sending a guest to the hospital for stitches and a tetanus shot was the last thing we needed. Even when rusted, the nails would certainly poke through the flimsy slippers most people wore.

The Jones' arrived back from their shopping excursion a few hours later when I was about done. I sat on the front steps for a break while I nurtured a glass of iced tea Auntie brought out for me. A heap of broken planks littered the ground to my right, waiting to be hauled away by Tad later in the day.

Mr. Jones struggled to carry stuffed bags filled with his wife's prizes for the day. I guessed their little shopping adventure cost him nearly a thousand dollars, more money than I had to my name.

"Be a dear and help my husband with our bags, would you?" Mrs. Jones said as she walked by me. She held her nose up when she looked at me. I was a mess, with my knees stained with dirt and my clothes saturated with wood flakes and dust. As I worked that morning, I tore a few holes in my jeans and t-shirt. I needed to buy new clothes. And that meant I needed to find a job.

It was bound to happen sooner or later. Auntie certainly couldn't afford to pay me, and I didn't flee to Maui to spend all my time being her chore boy. As Mr. Jones unloaded his bags into my arms, I wondered what I could do for work. I resolved to clean up and set out that afternoon to buy new clothes and job hunt.

I hauled the bags upstairs and followed Mr. and Mrs. Jones. Expecting them to turn left to the guest rooms, I was surprised to find they took Auntie's old apartment next to mine. Then again, it was the only room in the house with a five-piece bathroom and a kitchenette. The other rooms only had a toilet, sink, and a bathtub or standing shower.

I unloaded the bags in the small hallway leading further into the apartment. "Is there anything else I can get for you?" I asked Mr. Jones.

He shook his head and escorted me out of the room, slapping a crumpled up ten-dollar bill in my hands before he closed the door.

"How much did you tip him?" I heard his wife whisper from behind the door.

"Ten dollars, why?"

"That's much too much. He just carried our bags up."

"But look at him? He's poor."

"Please, he's a low life. Just look at that black eye he has. He must have gotten it in a bar fight or something."

I clenched the bill in my hands. Every bit of me wanted to burst through the door and tell the woman off. I heard her husband shush her.

"Be quiet. He could hear us." I heard the two of them rustling through their shopping bags.

"Don't take any of it out of the bags before we recheck the mattress. This looks like the kind of place that has bedbugs. Honestly, I don't know why you insisted we stay here without checking the other hotels first."

I didn't linger to listen to the rest of the conversation. I hated that Auntie reduced herself so much to accept these kinds of guests. I wished we could fix the place up enough to compete with the larger hotels so that Auntie could attract the sort of guests who wanted to stay here.

I walked into my room and closed the door, careful not to slam it. I didn't want the Jones' to know I heard them talking, although I could still hear their muffled conversation through our adjacent windows.

Peeling off all my sweaty clothes, I stood in the window and let the refreshing breeze wick the sweat off my skin. I enjoyed the fact that the window sill was at waist height. I could be naked in my room without anyone from the beach knowing it. To them, I might look like another tourist in a bathing suit.

Immediately below my room, the kitchen exited to a relaxing patio with a few wooden lounge chairs, a table, and a rocking chair I knew Auntie loved to use. Only a few dozen steps away, a rickety wooden walkway extended over an embankment and out to the beach where a family of tourists staked their claim for the day. A man and woman sat on a blanket with a large umbrella shading them from the sun while their child, a little girl, played by the shore. They watched over her dutifully. Her father joined her as she waddled deeper into the water until each wave came up to her waist. The girl looked only four or five. While kids raised on the islands comfortably ventured further into the waves at her age, I guessed she was hardly a strong swimmer. Most tourists weren't.

A group of rowdy teenage boys passed by the family. They kicked up sand, play wrestled, and talked too loudly to one another. One of the boys spotted me standing in the window and whispered to his buddies some joke, most likely about my too-scrawny torso or how I must have been "checking them out." I retreated into the bathroom and turned on the shower. The pipes rattled in the walls until the shower-head spat out water that took a minute to reach the right temperature. Twenty minutes later, I was cleaned, dressed in my only other change of clothes, and downstairs searching the reception stand for Auntie's car keys.

Auntie still sat in her chair in the window reading that day's newspaper, her thin-framed cheaters pinching her nose as she held the flimsy paper a few feet from her face.

"Are you going into town?" she asked.

"Yes. Can I take your car?"

"Only if you fill the tank." She peered up at me from behind the newspaper and raised a dangling set of keys in the air.

As I went to claim the keys, I spotted a white van in the parking lot. A group of suited men stood outside, holding a set of developer plans out in front of them.

I took the keyring from Auntie and rushed outside. She called out after me, but I ignored her. The men had no right to be here. They were like vultures. The property wasn't even theirs, yet they acted as though they already owned it.

"You're not welcome here! This is private property!" I yelled at them as I bounded down the front steps. One of the men looked up at me and cracked half a smile. As I approached them, I saw Tad's truck careen into the parking lot.

"If you don't want us here, call the police. Oh, wait. They won't do anything," the guy joked. He was a little spit of a man, hardly five feet tall, sporting an ugly tie and pants too big to fit his lanky frame. And he had the ugliest comb-over I'd ever seen.

As I got close, Tad's truck screeched to a stop. He nearly fell out as he struggled with a baseball bat in his hands.

"What did I tell you?" he yelled at the men and charged at them, threatening them with the baseball bat. Where the men didn't take me seriously, they seemed afraid of Tad. He banged the bat into their van as he approached.

"Get out of here before I get angry again!"

The men tried to roll up the plans, but Tad ripped them from their hands and crinkled them up. One of the suits tried to get them back. Tad pushed him away much too hard. He stumbled back and fell into the van's side door.

"Tad, stop!" I heard Auntie yell from the front porch. She held onto a support pillar in one hand with a cane in the other, trying to get down the stairs. I worried she might fall trying to get down too quickly. Tad seemed to worry also, and backed up from the men, ordering them off the property one more time.

We jogged back to the house as the van peeled out of the parking lot. Auntie looked pissed. She swung her cane at us as we tried to calm her down.

"You," she pointed the cane at me, "go away! We'll talk later. And Tad, how many times have I asked you to leave those men alone! Get inside! Now!"

I tried to speak up, to ask how long these men had been eyeing her property, but she wouldn't have it. So I left her alone and rounded the side of the house to the car, a jalopy if there ever was one. I sat in the car and gripped the steering wheel while I worried Auntie wasn't telling me everything.

Is it normal for developers to plan a whole project for a property they don't already own?

As I turned on the car and shifted it into drive, it sputtered and popped. The vehicle smelled old and stunk of burning chemicals as though it might overheat at any minute. Bits of it rattled as I drove it through the bumpy parking lot. It settled down as I pulled out onto the road and, with the windows down, the burning smell abated.

Turning left onto Honoapiilani Highway, I headed north. After a brief stop at a gas station to top up Auntie's tank, it took only ten minutes for me to reach Whalers Village, where I hoped I might look for work. As I walked through the modern shopping complex, I became nervous. I got my last job at the gaming shop only out of luck. My high school buddy was leaving for college and recommended me to replace him.

I walked to store after store where I was either scoffed at or politely told, "Sorry, we're not hiring now." I regretted not buying new clothes first. Faded jeans, ratty sneakers, and a worn t-shirt didn't offer the best impression. And my never having even interviewed for a job before showed.

At the very far end of the top-level, I smiled when I found a comic book and gaming store.

This is something I know I can do.

But I was wrong. I walked into the much-too-cold store to spot mostly empty shelves and table games so old they hadn't been mainstream in decades. As I made my way to the cashier, I looked through their Dungeons and Dragons section. The man still had version 3.5 stocked with no sign of the updated player's handbook, dungeon master's guide, or monster manual. I wasn't one to play much D&D, but I wondered why he didn't at least stock the 4th or 5th editions.

Next to it, he had a bunch of starter boxes for *Settlers of Catan* without any of the expansions or scenario box sets. The owner's card wall only featured *Magic: The Gathering*. I wondered if he stocked so few products because of an absent community on the island to buy them or if he simply didn't know what to sell.

I guessed the former since the store only had one other customer, browsing through comics in the back corner. The person I imagined was the owner waited patiently at the register, reading some science fiction book. He was a skinny, middle-aged man with thick-rimmed glasses too large for his face. He reminded me of my old boss back in Atlanta.

"Excuse me, sir?" I asked. He peeked up at me but didn't take his attention away from his book. In a glass case below him, several collectible comics and figurines were haphazardly arranged with small paper price tags attached to them.

"I was wondering if you're hiring."

The man sighed and closed his book. "No, I'm not. Are you going to buy anything?"

I looked around the cold, dark store. I was sure I could find something to buy. I just couldn't afford to spend right now.

"Sorry, no."

He turned his attention back to his book, completely ignoring me rather than enticing me into a purchase. *What an asshole.*

I left the store, the last one in Whalers Village, and decided to check out the beach. This area of the island sported the most picturesque views. In the afternoon, after the haze burned away, one could easily see Kaho'olawe, Lanai, and Moloka'i across the waters. To me, it felt like a magical archipelago, a home to countless adventures, myths, and legends.

I passed some restaurants and bars, but I knew from hearsay they rarely hired people like me off the street, especially with no restaurant experience. I thought about applying for the catamaran cruise company, but I had zero boating or entertainment experience.

Around me, tourists fluttered from one shop to the next, stuffed their faces with rich island food or Asian cuisine, or drank at a bar. They tossed money around left and right, willing to pay exorbitant prices to chain stores and tourist traps. I just didn't know how to get my hands on any of that money.

"Fuck," I mumbled to myself. Standing in the middle of Whalers Village surrounded by a horde of hyper vacationers made me feel out of place. For the last two decades of my life, I dreamed about returning to Maui and how comfortable I would feel once I got there. Instead, I felt like a minimum wage busboy at a black-tie gala surrounded by intangible wealth. When I was a child, I never grasped that aspect of the island, the part where tourists reigned supreme, and locals were trodden underfoot.

Auntie understood it. Tad sure did. The smile on his face after finding a free coconut proved that. As a child, I supposed Auntie and my mom made sure I never had to see this side of their lives, the part where they struggled to make ends meet while everything around them became more expensive, including the very land they owned.

A loud wedding party danced by, their winter-pale skin turned red from a day in the sun. I felt an urgent need to get out of there. I came to Maui to escape these people. I walked back to the parking garage. As I reached my car, my phone buzzed. I flipped it open and read a message from Tad:

Bro, Auntie said u was looking 4 a jb. Tlk to Jim @ Safeway. He hook u up. -T

Another text message came in — a list of groceries with every other item in the list misspelled. Tad wanted me to pick them up at the market. A group of teenage girls walked by me as I leaned against my car. I pocketed my phone and jumped into the driver's seat after they whispered to one another and giggled, making fun of my flip phone. They paused long enough for one of them to hold out their too large smartphones attached to a selfie-stick and all formed duck lips while they took a selfie. I wanted to take the stick away from them and snap it in half.

As I left the parking garage, I handed my voucher to a young ticket taker. "That'll be twelve dollars," he said.

I pulled out my wallet and mulled over handing him a twenty but he scratched his cheek, then tore up my ticket and raised the gate.

"Sorry, brah. Locals park for free," he lied as he waved me on.

Forty minutes later, thanks to evening traffic, I walked into the supermarket to the sound of Ed Sheeran's "Thinking Out Loud," barely loud enough to hear. I grabbed a cart and got to work roaming from one aisle to another as the song followed me. With a basket full of eggs, meats, veggies, fruits, pancake mix, bread, cold cuts, and other things, my fond memories of my childhood suddenly shattered when I landed on the last item in the list, POG concentrate. And in the juice section, I exchanged the childhood joy accompanying every single "hand-squeezed" glass of POG juice for a chilled, ultra-thick concoction of lies. The red carton sported an anthropomorphic pineapple with Mr. Peanut-like, white-gloved hands standing on a surfboard. Mr. Pineapple seemed to taunt me for daring to think every glass of my beloved POG was hand-squeezed.

I felt appropriately sad, like a child learning there was no Santa Claus, loaded my cart up, and made my way to the checkout. There, a pimply-faced teenager with a tan shirt, black shorts, and an apron rang me up.

"I'm looking for Jim. Is he around?" I asked.

The kid pointed at a man hovering over a small podium with a highlighter in his hand. He was a few years older than me, Tad's age. I guessed they went to school together. I paid the tender in cash and collected my groceries before I rolled my cart over to Jim. He spotted me as I approached.

"Sir, is there anything I can help you with?" he asked.

"Yeah. I'm Adam Frost, Tad's cousin. He told me to speak to you about a job?"

"Sure did, boss!" He warmed up immediately and waved me behind him to an employee break room just off the store's front end.

"Lucky Tad called me when he did. We let two guys go today. Fools didn't show up to work! If you'll show up on time, work hard, and treat customers good, the job's yours!" Jim sounded too happy, like he had a perpetual sugar high.

"What will I be doing, exactly?"

"Well, what won't you be doing? You'll work for me in the front. We'll start you out bagging groceries, collecting carts, emptying the bottle returns, and generally keeping the store clean. What do you say? I can start you out at $10.10 an hour for 25 hours a week."

The job offer was literally the best I had all day. It was certainly better than the $7.25 an hour I made back in Georgia.

"When do I start?" I asked. I was pleased with the offer. Not only would it earn me some pocket money, but it was within walking distance of the inn. I wouldn't have to burn through Auntie's gas or kill her car to get to work.

"What do you think about Thursday?" Jim pulled a clipboard off the wall with a schedule chart on it. He penciled my name in. "I can have you on a 9 a.m. to 2 p.m. shift. Can you show up around 8:30 to fill out the application and employment forms?"

"Application form?" I asked.

"Yeah. Boss doesn't like me hiring off the street like this. A proper application form will put his mind at ease. Don't worry, though. He won't even notice you. The guy spends most of his days locked up in his office in the back of the store."

The loudspeakers chirped, and a crackly voice filled the air. "Jim to the front end, please. Jim to the front end."

Jim put the clipboard back on the wall with my name written in tiny letters above a crossed-out former employee's. "Duty calls," he said. "See you first thing on Thursday."

"Wait! What do I need to wear?" I asked.

"Black pants and a black, v-neck t-shirt. We'll fit you with company shirts and an apron when you get here!" he said, then he sped away to the registers leaving me with my cart of groceries now very much in need of refrigeration. Already, a carton of ice cream on the very bottom of the list, most likely added by Tad, started to bulge as though it would rupture and leak at any moment.

I smiled, pleased with myself, and grateful that my cousin hooked me up.

I've got a job!

4
_____

DAY 5

AUNTIE WANTED LITTLE TO DO WITH TAD AND ME WHEN WE SHOWED UP for breakfast. The dining table was filled, Auntie now fixed firmly at the head of the table where she belonged with the Jones family at her side.

The night before, new guests checked in, the family of a local friend who needed a place to stay a few nights while they moved house. I recalled guests like these when I was a child. They fluttered in and out of the inn like birds looking for a perch, always taking advantage of Auntie's kind nature for a cheap roof over their heads and warm food in their bellies.

Today, those roosting birds included an older gentleman, his adult daughter, and two snot-nosed children who spent half the morning chasing one another around the inn screaming bloody murder. Tad leaned against the wall near the guest sign-in stand, his arms crossed, an angry expression on his face.

"You see this?" He gestured to the guest register as I came downstairs. Laughter exploded from the dining room as the older gentleman entertained a disinterested Mrs. Jones with a tawdry story of his ocean mishaps as a young boy growing up on Maui.

As I turned the registry over, I felt a sudden headache coming on.

Scrawled in Auntie's shaky handwriting, the names of our guests corresponded to the rooms they occupied. Of the twelve guest rooms we had, the family occupied four. A big X was penned in with Auntie's initials next to it on the room-rate column along with NA next to their checkout date. I wondered if it was a mistake, so I used the small key Auntie gave to me to open the key box hanging on the wall.

Sure enough, the guest copies for the four rooms were missing.

"She's not charging them?" I asked.

He huffed and pulled me into the kitchen so the guests couldn't hear us. "Oh, she's charging them, that's for sure. They paid in overripe fruit, liquor, and half a bottle of laundry detergent."

"So… they're costing us money?"

"That's an understatement. They're eating a mountain of food, taking crazy long showers, and the kids already broke one of the beds."

I mulled over the situation as I grabbed and started eating an apple banana, enjoying the acidic, apple-flavored banana not found on the mainland. I admired Auntie's charitable nature, that was for sure, but now was no time for charity when she risked losing her home. It would be different if the guests paid some small amount. Losing money on them was an entirely different matter.

"I'll talk to her later. We can't exactly kick them out now that they're already here. Auntie would kill us."

"That's for sure. Maybe she'll listen to you. God knows she don't listen to me."

Tad stormed off in a tizzy. Moments later, I heard his truck peeling out and speeding away. The older man in the next room, sitting directly across from Auntie, belly laughed again. I left the kitchen in time to see one of the kids, hardly four years old, tip over his glass of juice and stain Auntie's white tablecloth. She didn't seem to mind as the young woman sitting next to her father mouthed an apology and started dabbing up the juice into a white cloth napkin.

Mr. Jones, Auntie, and the older male guest seemed happy. Mrs. Jones sat there silently, poking a cold heap of scrambled eggs with her fork, waiting for her husband to finish so they could get out of there.

I needed to talk to Auntie. But not now. I didn't want to upset her in front of her guests and friends. So I slipped my sneakers on and left, first to Cannery Mall to get some new clothing, and then for an afternoon in Lahaina Town. There was undoubtedly no repair work for me at the inn that day. Not with two kids running around destroying everything in their path.

The morning was hot. Too hot. An "it's going to rain soon" hot. The sun blazed overhead, despite the dark storm clouds hovering over the mountains only a few miles away. I hoped the storm wasn't strong enough to make its way into town. The last thing I needed on a day out on foot was a soaking.

I lucked out. It only started raining just as I walked into the indoor mall, shocked by the rapid transition from hot, humid air to the brisk cold of an overused air conditioning system.

The mall only had fifteen clothing stores, half of them for beachwear or women's wear. Still, I found several items I needed: a new knapsack, new shorts, shirts, a bathing suit, two pairs of black pants, and some black v-neck undershirts. I cringed as I watched my wallet get thinner and thinner as cash practically flew into the hands of too-friendly cashiers. I almost regretted not taking Auntie's car to the outlets near the airport, where most locals shopped. I might have saved myself $100 if I went to a big-box store instead. However, I detested the idea of paying even more money to mega-corporations that tended to suck revenue off the island in exchange for cheap clothing that wore out after a few months.

With my brand new knapsack wrapped around my shoulders, nearly bursting with new clothing, I made my way down the now damp Front Street, the town's main tourist road, glad the rain had stopped.

I wanted to get reacquainted with the city I once called home. So I walked by one mixed plate restaurant after another, by Luau schools and outdoor theaters, and by too many snorkel and swimwear shops to count. Snorkeling sounded like fun if only I had the money to make it happen. Sure, Tad would let me borrow his gear, but his head was too big. And so was his mouth.

With only a few hundred bucks to spare, I settled for a nice cup of mango water ice and parked myself on a bench in Lahaina Banyan Court, admiring how bustling the downtown was, at least for a

Tuesday during the off-season. Ignoring the streams of tourists around me, I zoned out while spooning slushy into my mouth. Banyan Court made me feel truly at home. The massive tree covered half an acre and was over fifty feet high, its giant limbs growing horizontally and vertically with thick vines hanging down from the canopy. The tree possessed a mystical quality. Everyone, including children, knew it was something special. Despite being a tree-climbers paradise, no one dared climb it for fear of harming the tree.

Scattered throughout the square, local artists started setting up tables again after the brief rain, removing plastic from their tropical-colored canvases of magentas and aquas and blues and greens.

This part of Lahaina exemplified paradise, although the ever-growing crowds of travelers left me uneasy. Back in Atlanta, Jeff rarely let me go out. And when he did, even when in a crowded place, he had no problem making me feel like crap. "Why can't you look like that guy?" he would sometimes ask when an in-shape gym bunny passed us. Or, "Why waste MY money on crap you're not going to finish?" when the money also happened to be mine. I stupidly allowed him to deposit any money I earned into a joint checking account and wasn't permitted a debit card or checkbook.

Thinking of Jeff Thatcher spoiled my mood. It even soured my water ice. The sweet taste of mango turned metallic and bitter on my tongue. As I walked across the square, I tossed it in a trash barrel. My phone buzzed. I flipped the screen up and read a new text message.

I'll see you soon.

My stomach clenched. The message came from an unknown number and a strange area code. I stuffed my phone back in my pocket, my palms already turning wet. Beads of sweat started to collect on my brow. For the first time in two days, my ribs twinged. Pain from my prior injuries broke through the ibuprofen I dosed myself with like clockwork.

I scanned the crowd for any sign someone might be looking at me. I jumped from one man to another until, a hundred feet away, I spotted a familiar figure. My stomach lurched. I felt as though I might hurl. The man had his back turned to me, but his broad shoulders, built frame, cropped haircut and black hair were familiar to me. I sneaked around the banyan tree to get a better look. Even from a distance, the man possessed Jeff's chiseled jaw, thin cheeks, and high cheekbones.

My heart raced, the gentle organ pounding and palpitating in my chest. I was on the brink of a full-on panic attack even after I determined the man wasn't Jeff. He had a fully grown beard and wore glasses, two things Jeff most certainly didn't have. I turned and fled, speed-walking through the streets back towards the inn. Every step I took back home required so much energy. The bag clinging to my shoulders felt as though it had rocks in it.

I couldn't make it back to the inn. I turned down a side street and found myself in the Puupiha Cemetery surrounded by tombstones erected in mounds of beach sand. I nearly banged into a crooked cemetery sign and tripped over a rusty chicken-wire fence as I hid behind an old palm tree with my back pressed into the scratchy bark.

I pulled out my cell phone again. It had been three days since Jeff last texted or called. Surely he didn't find me already. I bought the ticket with cash at the airport after paying cash for a taxi there. Only my mother and sister knew where I was.

I scrolled through my contact list and dialed a number, clutched the phone against my ear, and listened as it rang.

"Adam, honey? I'm still at work. Can I call you back?"

"Mom," I blubbered into the phone, "did you or Maria get a new number?"

All I heard over the line was static and silence.

"Mom?"

"No, honey. Why? Is something wrong?"

I couldn't hide the fact I was crying. My stuffed nose and trembling voice gave me away.

"I'm scared, Mom. I got a strange text. All it said was 'I'll see you soon.'"

My mom cleared her throat. I heard shuffling of papers and some banging around, followed by a door slamming.

"Honey, where are you? Are you with Tad or Ala?"

"No. I'm at Puupiha Cemetery."

"Why in God's name are you there?"

"I couldn't get home, so I turned down a street and..." I trailed off. "Mom, you didn't hear anything from him, did you?'

"Since you left? Not a peep. Your sister hasn't seen or talked to him either."

I wiped tears from my burning cheeks and did my best to clear my nose.

"Do you think he found me?" I asked.

"I don't see how. There's no reason for him to think you're not still home."

"I am home, Mom."

"You know what I mean. Do you want me to follow up with the police?"

I mulled the idea over. Getting the police involved required they check on Jeff. If they did, he would know something was up. As a criminal attorney, he had friends in the Atlanta PD who always fed him information. I suddenly felt like I was in witness protection. The island began closing in on me like a prison.

"No. I don't want to risk him finding out where I am. It's better not to get the police any more involved."

"Adam, you can't hide out the rest of your life. Sooner or later, you'll have to deal with this. Have you thought about talking to someone about it?"

I laughed a little, although that made my rib cage throb all the more. "I couldn't afford it even if I wanted to."

"Still, you can talk to Tad and Ala. They need to know what happened to you."

"Auntie doesn't even know I'm gay," I said.

"Oh, honey. She absolutely does. I told Ala ages ago."

I was a bit mad all of a sudden. Upset that my mom took it upon herself to out me to the rest of the family. "And she's okay with it?"

"Of course she is, dear. We're all ohana. And that means uncondi-tional love and support."

I suddenly felt able to breathe better. Maybe she was right. I couldn't always call her every time I had a breakdown. And Auntie and Tad were here for me as much as I was for them. I still worried that Jeff knew where I was, though.

"Mom, can you do me a favor?"

"Anything, dear."

"Can you drive by my old apartment tonight? Just to see if Jeff's lights are on?"

"Of course. You want me to go in and beat him senseless in the meantime? You know I'll do it."

I chuckled. Tension washed away from me as though I were suddenly in a hot shower. "No. Please don't. It'll just make me feel better knowing he's still in Atlanta."

"All right. Just promise me you'll take care of yourself, will you?"

"I promise." I let the line go silent for a few moments. "And Mom? I love you."

"I love you too, honey. I'll talk to you tomorrow."

I heard her breathing on the other side of the line. She never hung up the phone first. It was something she didn't do. I said goodbye and flipped the phone closed.

I shuddered after hearing rustling behind me and spun around. Where I first expected to see a person jump out at me, because that was how my mind worked, I spotted a chicken—a frightening, feral, man-eating fowl on the hunt.

I laughed some more to myself. With my panic abated, it was high time for me to head back to the inn. Auntie prepared lunch at noon, come hell or high water. If I weren't there to eat, I would find only scraps left in the kitchen thanks in part to Tad's voracious appetite.

I pushed thoughts of Jeff out of my mind and abandoned the old cemetery for busier roads. As I approached the inn and spotted a now-empty parking lot, I became quite pleased. I wouldn't have to share my meal with hotel guests. And that meant time to set Auntie straight about free rooms.

It wasn't her fault, after all, that her friends decided to move. They certainly seemed able enough to pay at least something for their stay, or at least reduce the number of rooms they occupied to a more reasonable amount.

Yes. Auntie and I would handle her new guests. Despite my mother's request, I wouldn't talk to her about why I came to Maui in the first place. I wasn't quite ready to tell her everything. She had enough on her plate.

I went inside to rest for the remainder of the day, one that seemed darker and less vibrant thanks to my freak-out. The moment the door rattled shut, Auntie called out from the kitchen. "Lunchtime!"

5

DAY 7

My conversation with Auntie two days before bore fruit. Not only did Tad and I manage to milk thirty dollars in tips from Auntie's guests, mostly from Mr. Jones, but we also talked to her friends, who agreed to pay for the damaged furniture.

The night before, they decided they would buy and cook breakfast for all of us, including the Jones family, to repay Auntie for her kindness. I didn't get to enjoy it, though. With breakfast served at 9:30 a.m. and my needing to be at the supermarket at 8:30, I rolled out of bed with just enough time to shove a cereal bar in my mouth as I sped out the door.

No one was even awake. As I stumbled down the parking lot toward the main road, I hoped the market had some form of coffee in the break room. I sure needed it. Mr. and Mrs. Jones kept me up well past midnight with the moans and grunts that suggested they were really enjoying their vacation.

I strolled into the supermarket with five minutes left to spare, pleased with myself for being early on the first day of my brand new job. A half-asleep Jim waited for me at the podium in the front, forming only a half-smile when he saw me.

He covered his mouth to yawn as I approached. "Glad you're early.

That's more than the last guys could manage. Go in the break room and finish this paperwork while I sort out shirts and aprons for you."

He handed me a clipboard and strolled away, tripping over his feet a little in the process, leaving only a lonely cashier working the entire front end, a line of seven or eight cash registers, all but one closed for business.

I slipped into the break room, enjoying the smell of coffee in the air. On the opposite wall, a pod coffee maker beckoned to me. In front of the pods, a coffee tin labeled "Honor System. $.50 per pod" waited. I didn't have spare change, so I slipped in a dollar bill, knowing I would certainly take a second pod over my break, slotted the plastic tub into the maker, set a paper cup down, and activated it.

While the coffee maker worked its magic, I began filling out the short form in front of me with a ton of mundane details from my current address to my social security number to past job experience. The form was already half-filled out by Jim with my position details, starting salary, and hour limits.

I reached over while I filled out the form and collected my coffee, drinking it down black. I cringed a little when the bitter infusion hit my taste buds but soon adjusted to the bold flavor and started to wake up at last, just in time for the break room door to swing open and Jim to join me.

"Good. You found the coffee. You'll need it today."

"Why? Is there something special about today?"

"Not at all. It's just orientation day. Follow me."

I handed him the clipboard as he rushed out of the room. He led me to a small alcove near the break room with a punch clock on the wall, tossed me a bundle of medium-sized shirts I looked like I might drown in, and a single black apron.

"These are yours to keep. Make sure to wash them regularly. I already put your name tag on the apron."

He showed me the tag and a series of numbers on the back, my employee tracking number. After walking me through how to use it to punch in and start my shift, he led me back into a closet-like room nearby with a single computer and a headset that looked ready to fall apart.

"I need you to sit here and follow every prompt you see. There's a quiz at the end of each section. Pay attention to the information. If you get too many answers wrong, you have to start the section over."

I sat down at the computer and looked at the list of sections in front of me, a daunting arrangement of fifteen different training modules. Jim mumbled something about checking in on me later before he left me to browse through videos on job safety standards, customer service best practices, sexual harassment, bagging groceries, parking lot safety tips, theft, loss prevention, and so much more. Ninety-five percent of what the videos contained was common sense, easy enough for even a monkey to handle.

It was nearly 11 a.m. by the time Jim returned, just as I was about to finish the final quiz. The door swung open quickly enough to startle me. I looked up from the computer screen to see a big grin on Jim's face.

"Good. Most of the time I leave new folks in here, they're on their phones when I check in again." He squinted at the computer screen, pleased to see my progress, and took the mouse from me. A few clicks later and the final quiz for a segment on theft prevention was finished, filled out in whole by him. He tossed me a mesh neon vest.

"Take fifteen minutes to have a snack and do what you need to do. Then I need you to round up the shopping carts in the parking lot. Stack them together, but don't push more than five at a time. It's company policy."

I didn't need a break, though. I had been sitting in a tiny, freezing room for hours clicking through slides and multiple-choice questions. I was eager to get outside and followed Jim out of the room and into the bustling market, with most registers open to handle an influx of shoppers.

Eager to escape the cold market, I slipped on my vest and went outside. I inhaled the sweet scent of flowers mixed with a pungent aroma of cooked meats from a burger hut next door. Knowing I had fifteen minutes to spare, I took my time walking around the parking lot, collecting trolleys strewn about, most already placed in tiny corrals by customers mindful enough to put the carts where they belonged.

I spotted Tad's truck in the back of the lot and looked for him, knowing he was about ready to head out of town for an afternoon shift working the ziplines. I spotted him sitting outside the burger shop with a half-eaten sandwich on the table. He waved me over as he downed the rest of it in one giant bite.

"Looking good, cuz," he said with a mouth half full of food. He took a swig from a glass soda bottle to help swallow the rest of his food.

"Thanks," I said. "It feels good to be working again. I thought I would hate working outside, but I kind of like it."

He began to rustle around in a knapsack on the chair next to him, pulled out a small tube of sunscreen, and tossed it at me. I fumbled to catch it but failed. The sunscreen dropped to the ground and a little lotion splattered onto the pavement.

As I picked it up, Tad laughed a little. "Just as clumsy as when you were little, huh?"

"Yeah. I've never been one for sports, although I did make for a passable soccer player in middle school."

"Really? What position you play?"

"I was quite a good bench-warmer. Some say I was the best." It was a bad joke. Tad cringing at me proved it. I sat down with him for a minute and began slathering sunblock on my arms, neck, and face. Already I could tell the time spent outside the last few days had started to change my skin. Despite my darker complexion, the years I spent working in a comic book store or hiding out in my room playing video games left me looking more like a white guy with a tan rather than half-native Hawaiian.

The tell-tale sign of sunburn shone on my arms. I guessed my cheeks and ears were also turning a bit red. I pocketed the sunscreen after Tad insisted I keep it and leaned back in the chair, closing my eyes.

"What time do you have to be to work?" I asked.

"In an hour. Thought I'd check on you. I wanted to make sure Jim was treating you right."

"I'm treating him just fine," a voice called out from behind me. I jumped in my chair, startled by Jim standing there.

"I can tell. You let all your employees lounge around all day?" Tad asked. He playfully joked with Jim. I guessed the two had been friends for a while, although I didn't recall Jim from elementary school.

"Leave your cousin alone. He's on a break." Jim spun one of the chairs around so he could sit in it backward. Resting his arms on the back of the chair, he arched his back to stretch himself. He reached across the table and claimed a handful of Tad's soggy-looking french fries. Tad swatted his hand away, but Jim was too fast.

"Come on, guy! I need all the energy I can get this afternoon. I have two tour groups coming in."

"All the more reason for you not to stuff your face. I'm surprised you haven't busted the zipline."

"It's tested for up to 500 pounds!"

"My point entirely," Jim joked.

"Come on, cuz, are you going to let your boss talk to me like that? I'm not that fat!" Tad feigned anger, his hands held up, pretending to defend himself.

"I don't know. You're quite a bit more portly than I remember you."

"Last time you saw me, I was ten!"

I started laughing. So did Jim. This time, Tad looked less like he was pretending to be angry. He seemed legitimately upset. I could tell we touched on a soft spot. I didn't think he was the kind of guy to be self-conscious, but then again, I didn't know my cousin all that well. He began to pack up his stuff and finish his food, eager to leave.

"Don't be like that," Jim said. "I'm sorry. Adam and me are both sorry, right, Adam?"

"Right." I added, "To be honest, I'd rather look a bit more like you. I was the one who was a skinny little fuck. If not for your pounding every bully that picked on me, I would have been a miserable kid."

"Damn right!" Tad said. He relaxed again and settled back into his seat.

Jim stretched one more time and stood up, turning his attention back to the parking lot and the store. "As much as I'd love to chat, I got work to do. See me when you're done out here. We'll have you bag groceries before you clock out."

He spun around to walk away but stopped. "Oh! And before I

forget, a bunch of us are going to Big Beach for a cookout later. Tad, you in?"

Tad shook his head. "No can do. I work 'til seven."

"Adam, how about you?" Jim asked. Tad looked at me, silently compelling me to go. He was right. I couldn't start treating Maui like my home again unless I began building a life here. Auntie and Tad, though great, couldn't be my only friends.

"Sure thing," I said.

"Great. We're meeting there at five. Just look for the red canopy when you get there." Jim sauntered off, back into the market, leaving just Tad and me. Tad looked at his watch and sighed.

"Time to go, brah. Just make sure when you park at the beach, you leave the car unlocked and the windows down. And don't leave anything valuable in the car."

I nodded at Tad as he stuffed the rest of his food in his mouth. Once he finished eating, he grabbed his things. "Also, have some fun, won't ya? You've been moping around too much since you got here."

"To be fair, I was injured."

"Yeah. Are you ever going to tell me about that?"

"Maybe in a bit. I just don't want to talk about it right now."

"Well, if you need me to go to the mainland and beat the shit outta anyone, you let me know." He looked like he wanted to say more but stopped himself. He said his goodbyes and left, leaving me with a pile of his trash on the table to throw out.

By the time I finished clearing the trash and the rest of the carts in the parking lot, I only had thirty minutes left on my shift. I finished it out bagging groceries. My last order of the day involved an old biddy in a heavy raincoat who seemed to know I was new. She inhaled through her teeth every time she felt I did something wrong, either making the paper bags too heavy or putting her precious produce in the bag in some nonsensical order.

I held up my hands in surrender when she took over for me, pulling all the contents out of the final bag to make sure I didn't put her loaf of white bread on top of her precious tomatoes.

"Don't worry about it. Some of our customers are just like that. They complain about every little thing," Jim said as we walked to the wall clock. "I'll see you tonight," he added as I punched in my code to end my shift.

"Looking forward to it," I said to him, but he was already gone, speeding back to the front end after being paged. I was back in the parking lot at the inn in less than ten minutes, pleased with myself after having finished my first day of work, albeit a very short shift. I couldn't wait for my first paycheck and wondered how much of it I would use to make improvements to the inn.

So many things needed improving, from the landscaping to the front porch to the gray and chipping shutters. The entire front of the house needed a good sprucing up so I could take new pictures to advertise online and bring in real guests, not these second-hand rejects from other hotels or folks leeching on Auntie's kind nature.

The parking lot was empty, save Auntie's car parked at the side of the house. I climbed the steps and went inside, looking around for any sign our guests were present. I heard none. Looking at the guest register, I noticed her friends had checked out. Auntie stuck a note on the corkboard next to the podium with their room numbers on it, rooms I needed to clean sometime soon so we could use them for other guests.

I went to pocket the note and start cleaning, but a noise from the back of the house stopped me. I panicked after realizing it sounded like someone struggling. Flashes of Auntie wrestling an angry Jeff flashed in my mind for some reason. I nearly knocked over the podium on my way to the kitchen, fearing the worst.

Instead, I found Auntie on her hands and knees with a bucket and soapy sponge. She was straining, trying to get herself off the floor. Her cane was on the opposite side of the kitchen.

"Auntie! I told you yesterday I'd mop the floors after work! What are you doing?"

I slipped a little on the wet floor as I crossed the kitchen to help her up. Behind her, a nearly empty pitcher of juice sat on the ground. I guessed she dropped it and wanted to clean up the mess before anyone noticed.

"Don't talk to me like I'm an old lady!" she said as I helped her back to her feet. She proved more tired than usual, mostly from her exertion on the ground.

She set the sponge on the counter and started dusting herself off. "I needed to clean the floor before the ants came in. Anyhow, I would have gotten myself up eventually!"

"I wish you would have waited."

"Nonsense. I've been cleaning these floors every day for as long as I remember, and I will continue cleaning them until I'm unable to."

"Are you okay? Are you hurt?"

She took one look at me and smiled to put me at ease, although I thought I detected some worry in her eyes. She sat herself down in a chair at the kitchen table and motioned me to join her, a turkey sandwich and chips already waiting for me. "I'm not hurt. Sorry for snapping at you. I've become a dreadful old woman."

"Now that's nonsense. You're as kind and caring as I remember. Although, you've always had a bit of a temper."

She chuckled and then melted a little in the chair, resting her elbows on the table. "I want to be honest with you, though. It's the first time I've had trouble getting back on my feet since my fall. It did startle me a little."

"It startled me, too. I thought..." I stopped myself from continuing. "Forget it."

"You thought what? That your ex-boyfriend came here and was beating up on me like he did you?"

I swallowed a little as my neck tightened, worried about where the conversation was headed. "Mom told you?"

"She didn't have to. The moment I saw that black eye and the bruises on your arm, I knew what happened. You're not the first victim to recover under this roof."

I held her hand from across the table and swallowed again. I no longer felt tense. Auntie, knowing more or less what happened, put my mind at ease. "I love you, Auntie."

"And I love you too, Makani. I always will." She let go of my hand, pushed the sandwich plate closer to me, and got up from the table. "Now eat your lunch. You have some cleaning to do upstairs. If you need me, I'll be in here getting dinner ready."

"I don't need dinner tonight. A guy at work invited me to Big Beach for a cookout."

"That's great, dear! I didn't want to cook tonight, anyway. I'll just heat some leftovers and go to bed early."

"Are you sure? If you want me to, I'll stay with you."

"Don't be silly. Go out with your new friends. Maybe you'll meet a nice Hawaiian boy while you're out. It'll certainly stop you from moping around here all day long."

"You wouldn't mind? If I brought home a nice Hawaiian boy?"

"Certainly not! And if you want to impress him more, why not take my old room instead of that closet you have now?"

"Thanks, Auntie. I could do with some more space." My stomach rumbled loudly. I realized I hadn't eaten anything other than a cereal bar all day. Auntie laughed when she heard it and glared at my uneaten sandwich, silently ordering me to eat it. On her way to her bedroom, I could tell she was still shaky and wondered what it might mean to save the inn. The day when she could no longer manage it at all was approaching.

I thought about what that day might be like while I ate my meal in silence, lulled into a sense of peace and complacency by the sounds of the ocean waves breaking only fifty feet away. Was the Estate Inn without Auntie still the Estate Inn?

6

EVENING 7

LATE AFTERNOON TRAFFIC MADE ME LATE FOR THE COOKOUT. IT WAS 5:30 when I pulled into a half-empty parking lot on the edge of Big Beach. Disappointed revelers sauntered back to their cars with dry towels and dry bathing suits. Some towed upset children behind them who begged not to go.

As I parked my car and approached the beach, I spotted the reason for the mass exodus. A woman in a navy blue shirt and white shorts struggled to put up a giant red flag with a "No swimming" sign and a "Marine Stingers" sign affixed to the pole.

I stood at the entrance to the beach, my towel slung over my shoulder, looking for a red canopy tent. I wondered if Jim and the others got alerted ahead of time. I didn't see them and had no text messages.

The older woman working on the sign spotted me standing there.

"Local?" she asked me.

"More or less."

"The water's littered with man o' wars. You can use the beach. Just don't go swimming. I wouldn't even go near the shore if I were you. Some have already washed up."

"Thanks for the warning," I said.

She nodded and got back to work as I continued toward the nearly deserted beach. Some locals lingered, having nothing better to do, but all the tourists cleared out.

I spotted a group of guys climbing down a hillside on my right. One had a wet towel pressed to his arm. He cringed and hissed. I guessed he had an unfortunate encounter with a stinger.

They climbed the hill from Little Beach, the island's "most official unofficial" nude beach. Mom never let me go there as a kid. Understandably. We were raised by a Catholic father who insisted we adopt all of the rules and regulations and prudishness that came with it, from baptism to confirmation. I never got confirmed, though. My dad left us by then, despite the Church's stance on divorce.

I wondered what to do next. I could walk the whole length of Big Beach looking for Jim or I could throw caution to the wind and hike over the steep hill to Little Beach and lose my inhibitions. Mom would hate the idea.

"Don't go over there! It's littered with dirty hippies," she had once said to me when I was a child.

I didn't mind as much now, though. Dirty hippies seemed like they would be a fun bunch. It took me five minutes to climb through the steep, rocky ravine. I regretted showing up in slippers. The hike required sneakers, at a minimum. When I crested the hill, the walk down was a bit easier. I found myself at a much smaller beach, only a few hundred feet across.

The place looked nearly empty. Closer to the entrance, a few young women still lay on the sand, topless and without a care in the world. They shared a large bottle of beer between the three of them.

The girls ignored me as I walked by. Midway down the beach, an older couple packed up their things. They tried their best to put their clothes back on while minimizing the amount of sand that ended up in their trousers. Both of them smiled at me as I walked by.

"Don't go in the water. Too many jellyfish," the woman said to me.

Passing over her mixing up jellyfish with the Portuguese man o' war, I thanked her and continued to the far opposite end of the beach, now completely deserted. I spotted figures in the trees of hulking, naked old men perched in one spot or another hoping to cruise their way to a hookup. One of them noticed me and pursed his lips. I did my best to ignore him, hoping he might go away.

I admired them for their courage, though. What they attempted to do was certainly not in the Little Beach spirit, but that didn't stop them from cruising all day long. Illegal? Yes. Brave? For sure. The man ogling me got the hint that I wasn't interested and slipped back into the woods.

With him gone, I felt blissfully alone. I dropped my bathing suit, kicked off my slippers, and tossed them aside. After slathering some sunblock on my unmentionables — that part of me had never seen a moment of sunlight in my entire adult life — I lay back on the sand and basked in the late afternoon sun.

The waves, the brisk breeze, and the warm sand against my bare skin lulled me into a surprising sense of repose. I felt relaxed, more relaxed than I had ever felt in Atlanta. I closed my eyes and breathed deep the salty air, wearing nothing more than a lanyard with my keys around my neck.

At some point, the trials of the last week caught up with me, and the tranquil paradise around me soothed me to sleep. When I awoke again, the sun had set. I felt the sharp sting of sunburn setting in. It took me a few minutes to come to my senses.

How long was I asleep?

I felt my keys against my chest, the cold metal against my hot skin. For a few seconds, I was too groggy to move. I wondered if I was actually awake. I managed to sit upright and rubbed my eyes, careful not to get sand in them, then began searching for my swimsuit, towel, and phone. They were nowhere in sight. I struggled to my feet and combed the beach, thinking they blew away or were washed away by the approaching tide, but the sand around me was bone dry.

"Fuck," I muttered after realizing I had been robbed. I didn't care about my suit or towel, of course. I only had twenty dollars in my pocket for food and a few gallons of gas. My cheap phone wasn't much of a loss, either. My outburst was more like, "Fuck, I'm naked, in the dark, and a quarter-mile from my car."

I hoped no one set up camp on Big Beach or lingered in the parking lot, though. The last thing I needed was to be picked up by a cop for indecent exposure.

"Fuck!" I said again, this time louder. I stumbled as I walked further along the beach, looking for anything to cover myself. I even searched the treeline for any lingering cruiser who might lend me a towel. It was too dark to see. The new moon didn't help either. Absent its silver visage, all I saw were stars in the sky, too many stars providing too little illumination.

I covered myself with my hand as I walked to the cliffs to climb back over to the main beach. Without shoes, the climb up was challenging. Every few steps, my foot either slipped or stabbed into rough and jagged stone. I cursed with every painful step, recalling how easy this kind of climb was when I was a rough-footed youth on the island who ran around everywhere without shoes.

It took me ten minutes to crest the hill and climb back down. I scanned the beach for any sign of life. Midway down, I spotted firelight and wondered if I would find sympathetic locals willing to clothe me.

I knelt beside a boulder to get a better look, rubbing my hands against my battered knees. My palms suddenly felt moist. I'd scraped my skin on the climb enough to draw blood.

As I watched the fire from a distance, I realized it approached closer and closer. Then I heard drums and an odd chanting, I wondered if my eyes played tricks on me. I rubbed them some more, seriously questioning whether or not I was dreaming.

It wasn't a beach party, that was for sure. A line of figures, some holding torches, walked along the beach. No, they didn't walk. They practically glided. I counted ten figures in all, some banging on drums.

"What the hell are they doing? A reenactment?" I said as I sneaked along the sand to get a closer look. Only when I approached, I realized they weren't locals. They weren't tourists. Dozens of torches lit up, casting an orange glow across the sand. I estimated roughly thirty to forty people marching in a procession. Their eyes glowed ruby-red, and they carried bamboo spears and rudimentary weapons, most of them wearing nothing but loincloths, cloaks, and warrior helmets.

I knew then that it wasn't a joke. This was no reenactment. The stories my mom told me when I was a child came to mind. She always tried to frighten my friends and me with scary tales of the huaka'i pō, the Night Marchers, and their death-gaze. I did what any islander would do. I lay flat out on the beach with my bare ass in the air, covered my head, and squeezed my eyes shut as the marchers approached.

They surrounded me, I guessed. The beating of drums vibrated in my entire body. I trembled in the sand as they chanted a sorrowful, frightening battle dirge in a language I didn't know. The noise they made felt deafening, as though I were in the center of a tornado howling around me.

I felt sand cover my back and wondered if it was too late. Were they merely kicking sand on me as they marched? Or were they trying to bury me alive? Were they claiming me as one of their own, doomed to parade the island beaches and jungles for all eternity? I didn't dare look. I tried to control my breathing, but inhaling, even through my mouth, carried with it a death-like odor that made me gag. My heart raced. I started to whimper, then scream, just to hear something other than the pounding of drums around me.

Then it all stopped. The smell faded, the drums ceased, and the chant ended. All I felt was something cold prodding against my back. I struggled as I felt cold hands grab me and kicked and screamed, eyes still shut.

"Is he okay?" I heard a voice ask.

"Is he on drugs?" another chimed in.

"If he is, I want what he's having!" a third voice joked.

Figures around me lifted me to my feet. I felt weak, but they held me upright while I covered my hands with my face, still frozen and shocked.

I felt someone wrap a towel around my waist. The voice of a man called to me, comforted me.

"It's okay, braddah," a man said.

"Are they gone?" I asked, my hands still covering my eyes.

"Is who gone? You the only one here."

"The huaka'i pō. They surrounded me."

I heard multiple people gasp and suddenly felt embarrassed. I swallowed my fear and slowly opened my eyes. Five people stood around me, two women and three men. Two of the men still held me up while another, the oldest among them, stood right in front of me. He looked kind and spoke to me as though he had known me my whole life.

"No huaka'i pō here," he said. "We heard you screaming from the parking lot. Thought you were some shark bait swimming at night."

He handed me another towel to wrap around my shoulders.

"Thanks, Uncle," I said, making sure to be kind and respectful to the man.

"You actually saw huaka'i pō?"

I nodded, still somewhat out of breath, and proceeded to tell them everything I witnessed, from the drums to the smell to the clothes the marchers wore. I was still frazzled, though, and the group of them helped me back to my car. They told me to keep the towel around my waist.

Under the dull yellow overhead lights in the car, I closed my eyes and massaged my neck. I began questioning whether or not I experienced any of it or if, in a dehydrated stupor, I imagined it all. If I told Auntie what had happened, she might believe me. Tad, though, would laugh it up and slap my sunburned skin as a joke.

The air felt hot and stifling. Even with the windows rolled down, it felt more like summer in Atlanta than the chilly Maui evenings. As I leaned forward to put the key in the ignition and turn on the air conditioning, I winced. My skin peeled off the leather seat and sent jolts through my body. There was no avoiding what I had to do. I stepped out of the car and arranged the towel to cover the driver's seat and climbed back in.

"If I get pulled over, at least I'll have time to cover myself again," I said to no one. The car's engine sputtered a bit as I turned the ignition, before settling into a gentle rattle.

The digital display on the radio revealed the time. It was already 10:00. I had slept on the beach for four hours. Looking down at my junk, I knew the next few days would be uncomfortable. I looked like a cooked lobster. I cringed at the thought of skin peeling off certain areas of my body but knew there was no avoiding it. I was glad I didn't have to work the next day. Pushing carts with sunburn like this would have sucked.

With the roads empty, it didn't take me too long to get home. I made sure not to go over the speed limit. I didn't want to round out the night in a psych ward after telling the cops the Night Marchers stole my trunks. With the radio quietly playing pop songs from the mainland and the wind ripping through the car, I finally started to feel back to normal again and began tapping my fingers against the steering wheel and singing along.

I pulled into the inn an hour later and parked the car some distance from the house.

"Crap," I muttered to myself. There were about ten cars in the parking lot and lights on downstairs. Auntie, it would seem, decided to have a party instead of turning in early, the first since my arrival. I climbed out of the car and wrapped the towel around my waist, peering around the parking lot, looking for Tad's truck. He always kept it unlocked and last I checked, had some changes of clothes in the back. Only Tad wasn't there.

I crept closer to the house until I could look through the windows. I spotted clusters of people in the front parlor, some lingering in the hallway, and heard signs of activity from the back of the house. There was no graceful way to do this, so I bunched up the over-sized beach towel around my waist, making sure I couldn't trip over it and marched across the parking lot like a proud, barefoot, semi-nude dunce.

Just pretend nothing's wrong?

The front door squeaked a little too loudly and drew the attention of all the guests inside.

"Adam's home!" I heard Auntie say from the kitchen as she noticed me. With her cane leading the way, she walked into the front foyer. She stopped dead in her tracks after she saw my sunburn. "Oh, dear."

With everyone eying me, twenty to thirty guests in total, I panicked, apologized, and tried to scurry upstairs. Tripping on the towel only halfway up, I lost my balance and slammed into the steps. The towel fell loose and exposed my pale backside, the only part of me that seemed spared from sunburn, to the entire room.

I blushed, only I doubted they could tell. Any blood rushing to my cheeks matched the already deep red tone, and I scampered the rest of the length up the stairs, leaving the towel behind, until I was safely in my tiny room with the door slammed shut behind me. Sliding to the ground with my back against the door, I covered my face.

"This night can't get any worse," I muttered as I knocked my head into the door a few times. I reached down for my phone only to remember I lost it on the beach. I was just glad I didn't have too much money with me at the time.

I sighed as my stomach gurgled, lifted myself off the floor and found some clothes, wincing as I pulled on my loose-fitting gym shorts. Sitting on my bed, I closed my eyes and tried to slow my breathing. I could hear folks laughing from downstairs, having a good old time after I interrupted their party. Floorboards creaked in the hallway, then came a knock on my door.

"Go away!" I yelled.

"Don't give me that lip, Makani. Open up!"

Auntie's voice surprised me, not because she was checking up on me, but because she hiked upstairs to help me out. I reached over and turned the latch to unlock the door. It swung open to reveal a winded Auntie with a man next to her, holding onto her arm.

"Thanks, Gordon. I can take it from here," Auntie said. The man didn't say a word. He just looked at me, bemused, and shrugged, heading back downstairs to join the others.

Auntie came in with one hand guiding her cane and the other clutching a tub of aloe gel. She didn't look angry or upset. Instead, she smiled as though everything about the last few minutes was the highlight of her day.

Sitting on the bed next to me, she struggled to open the jar, passing it off to me to unscrew. "You want to tell me what happened? How my wonderful nephew left a few hours ago only to return as a sunburned nudist?"

"Not really," I mumbled.

Auntie scooped out a generous amount of aloe and started rubbing it on my shoulders. She slathered some on my hand as well so I could work on the front of my body.

"Let me guess. You found yourself at Little Beach at the end of the day and thought you'd take a nap under the sun? Then someone, most likely a beach bum, stole all your stuff?"

I nodded. I had nothing else to add. Auntie had an uncanny ability to get to the truth of things very quickly. I hissed through my teeth as she rubbed some aloe on my back. Her palms felt like ice against my flaming skin.

"You know, the same thing happened to your mother when she was your age."

"You're kidding?"

"No. Only she didn't have a car. She had to hitch a way home with some palm fronds to cover herself. Papa was furious. He didn't let her leave the house for a month."

"That really happened? She always told me she never went to Little Beach. She hates even the idea of it."

"She never told you why she hates it there?"

I shrugged.

"Because that's how she met your dad. He was the one that helped her get home."

"Seriously? " I couldn't believe it. Mom always told me they met at a party, not because he picked her up naked on the side of the road.

"It's true. She told me all about him when I helped put aloe on her, the same way I'm helping you now."

"So you're not mad at me for interrupting your party?"

"You mean for breathing life back into the party? Not at all. It was getting pretty boring before you busted in. Everyone's downstairs now telling their own stories about getting caught naked somewhere on the island."

She closed the jar, having covered most of my back, neck, and shoulders. "Anyhow, we shouldn't be talking about this. It's not my job to tell your mother's business, at least not without her here. For now, I need to get back to my guests. I suppose they'll all be leaving soon."

"Do you need help downstairs?" I watched her struggle to get back onto her feet.

"No. Going downstairs is fine. It's getting up that's the problem," she joked.

"Auntie, thanks for the help."

"Anything for my family, dear."

"And Auntie?" She stopped just in the doorway. "Please leave the jar. I still need it for—"

"That's right. Little Beach." She set the jar at the foot of my bed and grinned.

A minute later, I heard cheers from her guests. I figured they celebrated Auntie reaching the bottom safely. A booming man's voice shot upstairs. "A toast to our hostess!" he yelled in what sounded like a thick Scottish accent.

Before he continued, I closed the door and locked it, and got to work smothering gel on the rest of my body. Afterward, I was a sticky mess, the cooling balm soothing every inch of me. I opened all the windows in the room and let the trade winds work their magic. The combination of night air and moist skin had me feeling like I was in a cold shower.

I lay back on the bed and closed my eyes, hearing the sounds of cars starting and pulling out of the parking lot on the other side of the house. It was close to midnight, I guess, by the time I fell asleep.

7

EVENING 15

I SAT ON THE HOOD OF MY CAR AFTER A SEVEN-HOUR SHIFT, SCROLLING through dozens of text messages and hundreds of unread emails on my new phone. Splurging, I spent half of my first paycheck on a smartphone. Parked across from a Starbucks, I took advantage of their free internet while sipping on a Venti Iced Mocha, my drink of choice after I clocked out.

I got in the habit of messaging Mom on social media instead of over text, so I didn't have to pay to send it, and scrolled through my ever-growing list of contacts I began developing on the island. My friend feed was full of pictures of people's kids, their hobbies, their adventures, and general political nonsense that I didn't really care to read. At this time in my life, politics from the mainland didn't interest me much, although I sensed everything there was going to shit just by the tone of the posts I saw.

One political event did interest me, though. I received an invite from Gordon Wright, the Scottish man at Auntie's party a week ago, to attend a Maui County council meeting tonight. After a quick chat with Auntie over breakfast, I decided I would try to fight the balloon tax payment and ask for a reprieve for her since she was a native islander at risk of losing her home.

I worried all day about talking to the council in front of a large crowd. I hated everything about public speaking. The idea of it made my skin crawl. That feeling was only amplified by the buzz of caffeine working its way through my body. I had to stop drinking my coffee knowing full well it would leave me jittery for hours.

I threw it in a nearby barrel and climbed into the car, the backseat filled with groceries Auntie asked me to bring home. I noticed Jim sitting on a bench outside the market, talking to a girl next to him. He looked frustrated as she argued with him. After spotting me, he held up his hand to quiet her and came over to my window.

"What's up?" he asked me.

I didn't know how to respond. I just talked to him a few minutes ago. "Not much?" I asked.

"I don't really have anything to talk about, only my girl is arguing with me about her parents visiting this weekend. She wants them to stay with us; only our apartment embarrasses me."

"Okay," was all I could think of to say. He was getting to something. I smiled and waved at his girlfriend, surprised a bit that Jim even had one. It was stupid of me, but I initially guessed that he was single given the way he talked to other girls around the store.

"Do you think we could work something out with your aunt to stay at the inn? Perhaps put a little party together? I'd pay, of course, if you have rooms available."

I chuckled. "Yeah, we have rooms. Will it be just the four of you?"

"Five. Her little brother is coming too. How much you think two rooms will cost for seven nights?"

"Normal rate is $140 a room per night. But since you're booking two rooms, we can do $250 a night for both of them."

He shook his head. "That much, huh?"

"You won't find much cheaper."

"Come on. Do me a solid? What if I give you a raise? Say, an extra $1 an hour?"

"Now Jim, you're not trying to bribe me with company money, are you?" I joked.

"Only if it works. So what do you say?"

"Fine. $200 a night for both rooms, but you buy the groceries for the

64

party."

"Fair enough. We're picking them up from the airport on Saturday afternoon and can come right to the inn. You take cash?"

"Who in their right mind doesn't take cash?"

Jim pumped his fist. "Thanks, brah! You're a lifesaver! I'll see you on Saturday."

He returned to his girlfriend and talked to her for a few seconds. She jumped a few times and leaped into his arms, excited about the news, and the two of them walked back inside. In less than a minute, I was on the road, eager to get back to the inn. With my wounds all mostly healed and my ribs no longer twinging every time I rotated my torso, I had a ton of work to finish before I headed over to the county building for the evening meeting.

My plans for work were suddenly dashed as I approached the inn. The very same white van from the other week was parked in the middle of the lot. A crowd of men stood over a folding table littered with work plans. I turned into the parking lot and bounced forward as the car lurched to a stop. The gearshift stuck a little as I tried to put the car in park, so I set the emergency brake before getting out.

Auntie sat in a chair on the front porch. She looked concerned. As I climbed out of the car and walked toward the men, she called out to me.

"Adam, stop!"

I spun around to talk to her. She was on her feet already and started working her way down the front steps. "Auntie, they can't harass you like this! This is still your home!"

I started to shake a little. I hated confrontation like this. If I didn't have to worry about Tad attacking the men, I wished it was him here instead. Every inch of me wanted to run back in the house, but I fought against the urge and mustered up my courage.

"I thought we made it clear you're not welcome here!" Despite my voice trembling, I stood my ground. The men, three in all, snickered at me and continued discussing their plans. How was I going to make them leave? I certainly couldn't rip the plans away from them. I could tip over the table, but what would that accomplish? I knew I couldn't fight them.

"Who's in charge here?" I asked them.

"The boss is in the back," one of the men said.

The back of what? The van? The house?

I didn't need to wait to find out. The van shifted as a tall man climbed out. The sight of him overwhelmed me. I took a few paces back. By now, Auntie crossed the parking lot and stood at my side.

"Dad?" I asked. He wore a pressed suit that fit him perfectly, with sunglasses resting on the top of his head, almost hidden by his jet black, cropped hair. The only signs he'd changed were some noticeable wrinkles around his eyes and spots of gray around his ears. In the clothes he wore, I barely recognized him. If not for photographs that I kept while growing up, he would have seemed a perfect stranger. I hadn't seen him in over a decade.

"Good to see you, Adam," he said with a fake grin. "And Alana, nice to see you again."

I looked at Auntie. Her knuckles were white from clutching her cane.

"You knew?" I asked her. "You knew he was here, and you didn't tell me? Does Mom know?"

"I wanted to tell you, Makani. I just didn't know how you'd react."

I ignored Auntie for now. I was mad at her, yes, but I didn't want to argue with her in the middle of the parking lot. As for Will Frost, the father who abandoned my family, I didn't know what to say.

"Why are you here?" I muttered.

"Isn't that obvious? My company chose me as the project lead to develop this property. It's nothing personal, son. It's my job."

I clenched my fists, trying to bottle up my anger. "I'm not your son. You made that quite clear when you walked out on us."

He laughed a little and rubbed the back of his neck, as though disregarding me completely. "As I said, it's nothing personal. It's just business. You'll understand when you're older."

How can it not be personal? He is trying to take our home away from us. How could he be so cruel? Why did he accept this job knowing what it would mean?

All these thoughts raced through my head. I didn't have the confidence to say them aloud, so I said the next best thing.

"I think you should leave before I call the cops."

He raised his hands in the air and jokingly surrendered. "Fine. We'll leave, but you can't put this off forever. One way or another, we're going to knock down this shack and build some proper condos." Will signaled to his men to pack things up and climbed into the van.

Before they left the parking lot, he looked at Auntie. "And let me know about the offer I made. As I said, it doesn't matter to me whether I buy the land from you or at auction. My generous offer won't last forever."

I clenched my fist to prevent myself from lashing out and huffed at Auntie after they pulled out of the parking lot and disappeared down the street. As I turned around to head back into the house, she tried to catch my arm, but I pulled it away. I was upset. But when I turned around to argue with her about not telling me he was the one trying to take her property away, she looked dejected, as though every ounce of fight had left her body.

"Auntie, I'm not so mad at you that we can't talk," I said to her, rushing back to her side to take her arm and help her back into the house. "I just need honesty. I can't help you if you're hiding things."

"I know, Makani." At the top of the stairs, she took a moment to catch her breath. "I don't know why I didn't tell you. He's your father. You deserved to know. I just didn't know what to say."

My phone buzzed. I pulled it out to see the calendar reminder of the council meeting tonight, starting in less than an hour. I had to unload the groceries and leave in a few minutes if it meant getting there on time. "Well, we can talk about this later tonight. For now, I'm going to the county council meeting. Do you want to come?"

"Not on your life. I've argued with those people enough for one lifetime. Maybe you'll have better luck."

I helped her sit down and ran inside to change my clothes for the meeting. By the time I got outside again, she had dozed off. I didn't bother to wake her, considering she had no guests to tend to. We hadn't had a guest since Mr. and Mrs. Jones checked out.

After emptying the groceries into the kitchen, I hopped into the car, lifted the emergency brake, and turned on the headlights just as I pulled out of the parking lot. The sun was already beginning to set.

Long shadows cast over the road as I made my way to Honoapiilani Highway.

Forty-five minutes later, I pulled into the parking lot outside the county building and made my way inside. The half-empty lot betrayed the size of the meeting. I followed a crowd inside into what amounted to a theater-like council chamber, chairs already occupied by older members of the public with younger folks like me occupying the back and sides of the room.

Attending a local government meeting was a different experience for me. The last time I went to such a meeting was in high school, a requirement I had for a civics class. Shorter than most folks around me, I struggled to push my way closer to the front of the room so I could see, until I found a spot on the wall with an unobstructed view. The room felt hot, almost like a sauna. Elderly folks plopped their tired bodies down in uncomfortable chairs and waved themselves with fans, magazines, or pamphlets passed around with the meeting information.

Half of the overhead lights were off to make brighter a projector displaying the agenda on the back wall. The front of the room was brightly lit, featuring a row of wooden desks that matched the wood paneling on the wall behind the council members. Aside from who I guessed was the head of the council, the other elected officials had their backs turned to the crowd and could only be heard when speaking into their microphones.

For the better part of the first thirty minutes, all I heard were mumblings I barely understood about one project or another. A heated debate followed, with some audience participation on what new style of street lamps the county should purchase for Lahaina.

I smirked at a few older gentlemen in the front row, snoring loudly enough for everyone near us to hear. The head of the council, after a full hour of rambling nonsense, banged his gavel to open the room up to public inquiry. Chaos ensued as folks pushed one another to form two queues, one on each side of the room. Everyone present seemed eager to raise every and any complaint important to them. I managed to find a spot midway through the line on the left side of the room with four people in front of me.

"Please state your name," the counselor said to the older man at the head of my line.

"You know my damn name, Jerry!" the man coughed out.

"Noah, we've been over this. You need to state your name for the record."

"Fine. I'm Noah Wong."

"The chair recognizes Noah Wong. Please state your business."

"Well, let the damn record show that I think the council is doing a horrible job! I've been complaining about the broken street light on Kauhaa for a year! It still hasn't been fixed."

"That's because you haven't put in a request to public works. If you file the proper request, it'll get repaired in due course."

"Bullshit! You know requests to that department are like a black hole! I might as well fix it myself!"

The chairman banged the gavel and called for the next person in line from the other side of the room.

"State your name for the record," he said.

"Calder Wright."

The chairman yawned. "The chair recognizes Calder Wright. Please state your business."

The young man across the room looked familiar. I wondered if he was related to Gordon, perhaps his son. I stretched my neck out to get a better look at him, but only saw the back of his head.

"I'm here today on behalf of the Hana School Physical Education department. After putting in the proper request at the end of last semester, we've yet to receive funds for new equipment. I'm here to petition the council to vote on the release of three-thousand dollars from the general fund to better outfit our students."

The chairman covered his microphone and whispered to a young woman sitting at a desk to his left. The two talked for a minute while she pointed at something on her laptop before he returned to the microphone.

"My apologies, Mr. Wright. Funds for physical education have already been allocated for the year. It is not the responsibility of the taxpayers to foot the bill for your 'departments' inability to budget the money properly."

"But the money was spent to repair the roof! My students have none of the equipment they—"

The chairman banged the gavel. "You're out of order, Mr. Wright. Please yield the floor!"

Calder Wright protested, refusing to give up the microphone as he tried to plead passionately, but to no avail.

The chairman banged the gavel louder until those around him covered their ears. "That's enough, Mr. Wright! One more outburst like that and I'll have you removed from the chamber! Next!"

The young man sulked away from the microphone. I tried to follow him with my eyes, but he vanished into the crowd. I felt terrible for him and started to despise the chairman who seemed to exert totalitarian control over the entire room. As a few more people raised their questions or concerns, it became apparent the whole meeting was a circus, and that no complaint raised by any citizen mattered to the council.

"Please state your name for the record," the chairman said. He cleared his throat loudly enough to draw my attention. Realizing I was suddenly at the front of the line and he was talking to me, I froze. The anxiety of public speaking caught up to me, manifesting as a lump in my throat.

"Adam Frost," I tried to say.

"Louder, please."

I cleared my throat loudly enough that the microphone rang from the feedback. "Adam Frost."

"The chair recognizes Adam Frost. Please state your business."

"I'm here on behalf of Alana Manalo, and would like to discuss the possibility of granting an exception to her property tax balloon payment under current native Hawaiian land tax exemption laws, and submit the Estate Inn for recognition as a historic landmark."

"Objection!"

I spun around to a loud, familiar voice from the other side of the room.

The chairman banged his gavel. "The floor recognizes William Frost."

"Thank you, Mr. Chairman. I'd like to raise a motion recognizing Adam Frost as out of order. Not only does the land tax exemption law apply only to landlocked parcels intended for agricultural or residential purposes, but this is the wrong forum to raise what many deem to be a private matter between the finance department and a private citizen. Furthermore, unless Mr. Adam Frost is claiming to be a legal representative or executor for Mrs. Alana Manalo, he has no standing to raise issues on her behalf."

"Do I hear a second?" the chairman asked.

Before I could protest, another council member lazily raised his hand, and the gavel banged.

"The motion stands. The chair recognizes Adam Frost as out of order. Mr. Frost, please yield the floor."

I felt immediately fueled by anger toward my father. My cheeks burned, and my head spun. The fighter in me, however small, wanted to kick him in the nuts. The more passive side of me that flees in the face of conflict wanted to sulk away and hide in a corner, too embarrassed to show my face again.

I bolted from the room. Before I pushed my way out of the chamber, I felt a firm hand on my shoulder and looked up to see the big, bad William Frost, my absent father, grinning at me.

"Just tell her to accept my deal. She can find a nice hut somewhere on the other side of the highway if she insists on living here."

"Let go of me!" I used both my hands to shove him away with all my strength, hardly enough to send him staggering back more than a few feet. I heard whispers from those around me, shocked by the scene we created, and used the free moment to book it from the building into the parking lot where I could breathe again.

"Fuck!" I said as I kicked a nearby trash bin. The plastic bin fell over, spilling its contents down the stairs.

The cool breeze, the empty parking lot, and the setting sun were hardly enough to stem my tension buzz. I staggered down the stairs toward my car, breathing so quickly some might think I just ended a marathon sprint. I prepared for my fourth panic attack in the last two weeks, the former being my previous hallucination of Night Marchers on Big Beach.

At my car, with my arms resting against the roof and my face hidden from sight, I did my best to calm down, chasing away thoughts of how worthless I was, how I deserved all the abuse I received from Jeff, from my father, and how much of a disappointment I was to my family.

I felt another hand on my shoulder and lashed out. "I told you to leave me alone!"

Spinning around, prepared to lash out at my father, I was surprised to see the young man from earlier, the gym teacher, Calder Wright.

He jumped back from me, a bit freaked out, and raised his hands to block my swing.

He didn't need to. Realizing it wasn't my father calmed me almost immediately. My breathing improved, but the episode left me exhausted. I stumbled back into the car, then sank into a squatting position.

"I'm sorry. I thought you were someone else," I said.

He didn't respond. He just squatted in front of me. I looked him up and down. He was young, like me, with vibrant brown hair that didn't tame well in the island heat, his skin tanned after too much time on the island.

Most of all, he looked nothing like Jeff. Where Jeff had broad shoulders and a narrow waist, Calder was stocky, a little plump in an entirely appropriate way — less gym bunny and more weekend warrior. Jeff had a slender face and a sly grin. Calder had a rounder face, bushy eyebrows, and at the moment, a warm, albeit concerned half-smile.

"I saw what happened. Are you okay?" Calder asked.

"I've been better. How about you? You didn't do too well, either."

"Nah, but that won't stop me from coming back. I've been at this meeting every session for the last five months. I just can't wait for election day when I can vote against this jackass of a chairman."

I watched Calder while he spoke, paying particular attention to the unique way he formed some of the words with a slight hint of a Scottish accent.

"You're not from Maui?"

"My father moved us here for work when I was seven. You and I met before, you know, although I doubt you remember."

"What do you mean?"

"My family used to live in Lahaina before we moved to Hana. We were always over at your auntie's place for dinner. You were just a little kid then, no older than four or five. You were always too busy following Tad or your sister around to play with me, though."

"That sounds like something I would do. My sister and I were joined at the hip when I was that young."

I felt completely at ease again, more now that I knew we weren't total strangers, and felt a tightening in my shorts as Calder and I locked gazes.

I knew immediately he was into guys. Straight men don't share glances like that. You can't get a straight guy to look you in the eyes for more than a few seconds. They always seem too conditioned against the intimacy it implies.

"Come on," Calder said. "Let's get you out of here before the meeting ends. My dad told me you were staying with Alana? I take it you're going back there?"

I nodded as I fished my car keys from my pocket. "How about you? You're not driving back to Hana tonight, are you? That's a two-hour drive."

"Nah. I have a few couches I can crash on tonight on this side. Plus, I don't need to be to work 'til noon."

"Couches? Why don't you stay at the inn? We have plenty of rooms." I didn't know what came over me, inviting him over out of the blue. But as I looked up at him, now smiling from ear to ear, I knew I did the right thing.

"Sure! I'll meet you there. Thanks. I'm glad we ran into each other again."

"Same," I said as I turned the key in the ignition. The car rattled, popped, but failed to turn over. Another attempt produced similar results, and then it died entirely. Further tries produced only barely audible clicks. I slammed my palm into the steering wheel.

"Umm... You think you can give me a ride there as well?"

"Only if you don't mind a motorcycle."

I raised my eyebrows. The idea of me pressing against him for almost an hour made me twitch involuntarily. I hadn't felt this about anyone, even Jeff, in so long. My heart skipped a beat at the perceived flirtation and immediate attraction we seemed to share. I hoped he didn't notice what was happening in my pants. For once, I was glad I wore briefs and jeans rather than boxer briefs and shorts.

He walked me to his bike and handed me a spare helmet from the small trunk. Noticing I struggled with the strap, he took a moment to help me put it on, then straddled the bike, waiting for me to join him.

I hesitated. At that moment, the doors to the council chamber slammed open. A crowd of people began pouring into the parking lot. This drew Calder's attention long enough for me to reach down my pants and adjust myself in vain.

Fixing my pants proved a futile exercise. Whether I pointed it left, right, down, or up, I knew Calder felt it the moment I swung my leg over the bike and pressed myself into him. His trunk left me very little room to slide backward.

As I placed my hands on his shoulders, my groin pressed firmly into his back. He gave no indication that he noticed or cared. He just took one of my hands and placed it around his waist.

"Wrap your hands around me. It's safer that way."

As I settled my feet onto the passenger footpegs, I had no other choice but to oblige. Holding onto him like this was the closest I had been to another man in years.

Even Jeff and I never got this close. Instead, Jeff usually had me strip down, bend over, and take it on his schedule without caring about my pleasure. He certainly didn't like to cuddle, and came to bed drunk more times than sober. With so much space between us, it often felt like I shared a bed with a stranger.

But now, the novelty of Calder and my chest pressed into his strong back, with my hands wrapped around his stocky waist, I could barely contain my arousal. And it definitely showed. He definitely knew. There was no working around a stiff one pressed against his ass.

"You ready?" he asked as he fired up the beast between our legs. He cranked something on the handlebars that caused the engine to rev up, violently vibrating my legs. He laughed as I clutched him tighter and slowly pulled out of the parking lot. The last sliver of daylight slipped beyond the horizon, and the soft yellow street lights lit our way.

8

EVENING 15 - PART 2

As we sped down the highway, I tried to come up with words, any words, to describe how I felt. The ever-present anxiety over the inn, Jeff, my father, and money worries disappeared amidst a sense of numbness between my thighs, trepidation over my attraction to Calder, and euphoria as the island breeze caressed my arms.

With nowhere to put my head in my current position, I rested my cheek against Calder's back. He radiated a warmth that chased the chilly breeze away. I inhaled his scent of earth and sweat and sunscreen. I remembered a favorite episode of Doctor Who — Petrichor, the smell of earth after the first fat, wet drops of rainfall on a dry summer day, the smell of dust after rain.

His was a comforting aroma, an island perfume that entranced me and heightened my arousal.

"Lean into the turn with me!" he shouted over the roar of the engine. Speeding up through the final tunnel before the turnoff into Lahaina, he zipped by a tour bus filled with travelers weary from a long day of island excursions. As we switched lanes and zoomed by them, I spotted a child pressing their face into the window, waving as we passed.

Soon enough, we coasted by the ocean-side highway I'd driven a handful of times since my return to the island. I never really noticed how beautiful it was at high tide. I squeezed Calder tighter and shifted my weight into him, watching each wave crash against the rocky shore, splashing us with a warm, salty mist.

I leaned with him turn after turn, pleased with how synchronized and smart I felt riding a motorcycle for the first time. I wasn't scared of crashing or falling off. For some curious reason, Calder made me feel safe.

By the time we pulled into the crumbling parking lot of the Estate Inn, I was sad the ride was over. Calder put the bike in park and turned it off.

I realized how fast my heart had been racing the entire ride, and how hard I had been holding onto him, with my arms wrapped around his torso.

I lingered there, holding onto Calder for longer than I should have until he cleared his throat.

"Sorry," I said, letting him go. I swung my leg over and jumped off the bike, fiddling with my helmet as he set the kick-stand.

"Here, let me," he said as he fiddled around my chin. I heard a little click, and the strap released.

"Your first time on a bike?" he asked while he stored my helmet in his trunk bag.

"Could you tell?"

"Not really. I'm just glad you were comfortable being close to me. It makes riding much easier. Most guys try to sit as far away as possible. Makes turning the bike a bitch."

A few moments later, I led the way inside, beyond the pile of broken planks that previously made up the tattered picket fence.

Although I left Auntie in her chair before the meeting, it was empty, gently shifting back and forth with every small gust of wind. Inside, the lights were all off aside from the front hallway.

"No guests tonight?" Calder asked.

"Or last night, or the night before. We have a party of five checking in this weekend, though."

Calder joined me in the hallway from the porch. "That sucks. I can pay a little for the room if you—"

"Nah. I was going to put you in my old room. We don't use it for hotel guests."

"I remember. The tiny one in the corner, right? With all the trucks under the bed?"

Suddenly, a memory came to me. I recalled a much larger Tad with a ginger-haired boy about the same age playing with my trucks. And I remember wailing at them because I didn't want to share my favorite firetruck with them after the boy broke the ladder.

"I remember now! You broke my firetruck!"

"I'm sorry?" Calder offered a fake, jovial apology.

"You're lucky I'm in a forgiving mood tonight," I joked. The two of us awkwardly laughed away our lousy sense of humor as we sauntered into the parlor.

Calder claimed one of the loveseats near the entry with a plop and a loud sigh while I worked my magic on Auntie's liquor cabinet. Pulling out two glasses and a bottle of rum, I poured each of us a drink before claiming the only other seat near him, an overstuffed leather chair cracked and dried from decades of heavy use.

Swirling the liquor in the glass, I took a sip, realizing I was now getting used to the potent concoction. Instead of just burning my tongue and throat, I detected hints of ginger masked behind a sugary mouth punch.

Calder sipped from his glass like a professional, as though he had been drinking the rum all his life. We both poured ourselves another glass. I imagined neither of us was sure how to break the silence. I silently wished Auntie would rescue me from this tense moment, made worse by my ever-mounting attraction to Calder. Now, under the overhead parlor lights, it became apparent my appeal was justified.

In the dark parking lot, I didn't notice the faint trace of facial hair that, given a few more days, would grow into a full beard and mustache. Nor the thickness of his thighs and calves, nor the way his ginger sideburns faded into fluffy, vibrant brown hair.

All in all, he enticed me. We locked gazes again, and I knew he felt the same way. Sometimes, you just knew when things were mutual, like when you check out a guy walking by you in the street only for both of you to turn around, slow down, and linger long enough to psychically say, "Damn, you're hot!"

The second glass of rum in too-few minutes didn't help. My heart fluttered. I involuntarily tugged at my collar and cleared my throat.

I could feel my cheeks blush, and, for the second time that night, my pants tighten. The way he adjusted himself made it clear he was in a similar jam, although I guessed both of us were well out of practice and didn't know how to proceed.

I broke the silence. "When was the last time you were here?"

"In Lahaina or the inn?" Calder asked, taking the opportunity to sit further upright and adjust himself.

"The inn," I clarified, as I reached for the bottle to fill our glasses for the third and final time, emptying it completely.

"I pick my father up here all the time, although I haven't been inside for a while."

"Wait. Your father rides your bike with you?"

Calder laughed. "Oh, God, no! He'd freak out. He hates the motor-cycle. I usually only ride the bike around Hana, but my truck is in the shop. My parents don't like the idea of me riding my motorcycle on Hana Highway. All the twists and turns."

Calder tossed his glass and stood up a bit too quickly, wobbling back and forth to the dance of too much rum. "So," he said while he balanced himself, "care to show me around?"

He reached his hand out to me and helped me up. Like him, the alcohol rushed to my head. He stabilized me with a firm grip around my waist while I finished off my glass.

After a quick tour of the house, which was more like a fast pass through the kitchen, a moment of admiration of the ocean view, and my quickly glancing into Auntie's room to spot her snoozing in her armchair, we made our way upstairs.

I didn't need to tell Calder where to go. Both of us, driven by whimsy and rum, entered my childhood bedroom.

"It's a bit smaller than I remember," he said, poking his head in the small, three-piece bathroom.

"Well, we're both a bit bigger than we used to be."

Calder moved closer to me, invading my personal space in a way that caught me by surprise. "I've noticed."

His looming presence, although welcomed, triggered something in me that made me quite uncomfortable, in part because I didn't expect him to be so suddenly forward. I cleared my throat and stepped back until I stood in the doorway. It was my way to regain some control over the situation.

An image of Jeff invaded my brain, and the pain and psychological torment that usually followed came to mind. Now my heart raced for a very different reason.

I looked up at Calder. He seemed confused and dejected.

"I'm sorry," I said, rubbing and stretching my neck. The motion was one I was familiar with, a coping mechanism I developed to hide what had become a nervous tick, an inability to look people in the eyes when I felt uncomfortable. "You just caught me by surprise."

"I'm so sorry, Adam. I thought you felt the same…"

"I did. I mean… I do. It's just been a while. Can we, you know, slow down?"

Calder smiled and backed up a few paces until he sat against the window sill. The room between us made me feel more at ease. Although he seemed a little frustrated and still confused, he definitely possessed much more self-confidence than me. "Absolutely. What did you have in mind?"

"Well, I haven't been back here for very long. How about a tour of your favorite places on the island?"

He perked up, straightening his back and smiling. "Absolutely! I can show you all my secret places around Hana, places tourists don't go. Sounds good?"

"Sounds great. How about next weekend, once our guests leave?"

He nodded, and both of us were soon back to our semi-drunk selves. Now that I was in control of the situation again, I approached Calder. He was kind, friendly, and more than eager, given the tent he was pitching in his pants.

Considering he was taller than me by a good six inches, I stood on the balls of my feet to reach up to him and kissed him on the cheek. He blushed and rubbed where my lips had been.

"What was that for?" he asked.

"For being nice to me tonight. And for giving me a ride."

He returned the favor, slowly closing the distance between us. Being much gentler than a minute ago, he leaned down and kissed me on the cheek as well, a little closer to my lips. "You're very welcome."

A few moments later, both of us were alone. I could hear him banging around the tiny bedroom, preparing for bed. Knowing he didn't pack for an overnight, I wondered how he was going to sleep. Shirtless? Pantless? Wearing nothing at all?

Despite my brain telling me to slow down, my body screamed at me to speed up, to go back to that room and hop in bed with him.

Or was that just the rum talking? It wasn't long before I heard the squeaking of mattress springs through the wall, then nothing. If I wanted to spend more time with Calder tonight, it had to be in my dreams.

Peeling off all my clothes, lying down in nothing but my briefs, I pondered the implications of tonight as I watched the ceiling fan circle above me. The shadow of the fan blades spinning around the room hypnotized me.

Although I was more than attracted to Calder, the timing of it all couldn't be worse. I was only two weeks out of a years-long, destructive relationship. My finances were a mess, the inn was a mess, I worked a near-minimum wage, part-time job, and I knew nothing about Calder aside from the fact that he was a gym teacher and that he played with Tad when we were kids.

It didn't take long for my racing mind to quiet and for sleep to take me and chase away the stress and excitement of the day.

My last thought of the night was a pleasant one. As my second week on Maui drew to a close, I realized I was starting to live life again. I felt more myself now than I had ever felt in Atlanta. Tonight, as I raced on the back of a motorcycle down Honoapiilani Highway, I felt more myself than I had in the last fifteen years.

9

DAY 19

BREAKFAST WAS DELICIOUS. AUNTIE COOKED AS USUAL, AND A GOOD THING too. Since Calder left a few mornings ago, exchanging numbers with me, the two of us had spent most of the time flirting back and forth like giddy schoolboys. I tried cooking breakfast the morning he left only to make burnt oatmeal.

Auntie had no clue what was wrong with me. She had whipped a kitchen towel at me, demanding I get out.

That was Tuesday morning. Wednesday, Thursday, and Friday were about the same. We'd exchange selfies, joke about Tad, or work, or tourists, and talked about the one topic on everyone's mind since Tuesday, a forming hurricane that looked like it might miss the islands.

He had sent me one bold picture of himself at a waterfall with his shirt removed and draped over his bare shoulder. Because of the angle, it wasn't clear if he was wearing anything else. The picture did show his arms and pecs were as firm and well built as his legs, hardly unexpected for a young and active gym teacher.

"One of our stops next weekend," he wrote before sending the picture.

I was about to respond to the message when I heard a car pull into the lot. Tad was occupied with other chores around the inn, taking the time to finish construction on the wrap-around porch. Auntie had spent most of the morning on the back patio, suspiciously eying the horizon for any sign the hurricane might decide to pay us a visit. "It doesn't feel right," she told me when I found her out there at sunrise.

I had spent the better part of the morning going over the inn's accounts, adding in what meager money Tad and I could afford to part with to the overall sum owed in back taxes. Of the thirty-thousand owed, we currently had $4.5 thousand saved. That left us with another few weeks to make up the remainder.

Luckily, Jim's seven-night stay at $200 a night for two rooms, minus expenses, would bring the total up to $5.7 thousand. I was also planning a fundraiser event for all of Auntie's friends, despite her protests, and waiting for approval for an online fundraising page. However, I didn't add my name to it, worried it would circle around to Jeff.

Packing the papers away and running into the lobby, I staffed the check-in stand just in time to spot Jim struggling with too many suitcases for his wiry frame.

Behind him, his girlfriend—and I hadn't yet caught her name—and her parents and little brother followed. Seeing the way they let Jim struggle with the luggage made me immediately dislike them all.

Especially the little brother, who looked like a douchebag high-schooler if I ever saw one. It wasn't necessarily the flat-rimmed hat and nipple-showing tank top. I wasn't one to judge folks on their appearance.

It was the way he jogged up to Jim, tossed a duffle bag over Jim's shoulder, and ran away around the side of the house toward the beach.

This left Jim carrying four bags while his girlfriend and her family took none, save the mother's oversized Vera Bradley.

Tad came inside before they reached the house, giving me enough time to pry.

"Exactly how much do you know about these people?" I asked him.

"Enough to know they paying us $1400. We need the money, so be nice!"

Jim stepped inside. Dropping the suitcases with a grunt, he rolled his eyes. He already seemed done with his girlfriend's family for the day.

"Aloha! Welcome to the Estate Inn!"

Tad's boisterous greeting and his massive presence surprised the mother, who let out a yelp and jumped back into her husband. She placed her hand over her chest and laughed, as most people tend to do after being startled.

I slapped Tad on the shoulder. "Go finish the porch."

With Tad out of the way, I grabbed two guest keys and handed both to Jim. "Mr. and Mrs. Seren, we've laid out a spread for you in the parlor. There's also an open liquor cabinet and juice—"

"No need. Just show us to our rooms. Jimmy here can handle the bags."

Despite Mr. Seren's instructions, I took two of the smaller bags from Jim and led them upstairs. As I wound around the banister, I spotted an eager Auntie waiting in the parlor, ever-excited to meet her new guests.

I could tell she was upset from twenty feet away. The way her cane trembled under her tight grip spoke volumes more than she ever could verbally. These people rejected her tasty treats and ready-to-make cocktails hospitality. They were most definitely not ohana.

I reached the top of the stairs and turned left, winding my way around the plantation-style home until I reached rooms eleven and twelve. Not only were the two rooms ocean-facing, but they were as far away from my apartment as I could put them.

They claimed their two rooms and shut the doors, leaving absolutely no tip in my hand. The colorful vulgarities flying through my mind most likely sang in harmony with Auntie's.

A sudden crash from downstairs drew my attention. Moments later, I was helping Auntie and Tad pick up our little pamphlet stand, blown clear off the table by a gust of wind that surged through the house from the beach. More importantly, in the wrong direction. We were used to the wind blowing toward the shore, bringing with it colder damp air from the higher elevations of the island. But the sickly, warm bluster from the beach left us worried.

I'd performed this chore before, picking up rubbish after the wind blew it down, and knew immediately what I needed to do. One look into Auntie's eyes revealed concern above and beyond rude guests.

"I'll get the radio," I said.

After picking up the rest of the pamphlets and storing them away, the three of us secluded ourselves in the kitchen as Tad tinkered with Auntie's Lafayette portable radio. I'd say it was vintage, but it wasn't. It was an antique, a radio older than I was that managed to work better than any portable ones made today.

As Tad extended the three-foot-long antenna and pointed it toward the center of the island, another violent gust rattled all the windows in the house. I heard a slam from outside as a lawn chair bashed into the screen door.

My phone vibrated. Unlocking it, I read a text from Calder.

You all getting these winds? Road to Hana already closed. Can I stay over? -C

Of course. We're checking the weather now. See you soon! -A

"Calder's on his way. Hana Highway is closed," I said to them.

Auntie nodded. This wasn't relevant to her. Her home always had sheltered friends from the rain, especially those traveling from Hana or from other islands for the day. She returned her attention to the radio after Tad finally landed on a weather station.

Four loud buzzes echoed through the kitchen—a weather alert issued by NOAA followed by a loud chime and a robotic voice.

"A hurricane warning has been issued for Hawaii, Maui, Kalawao, Honolulu, and Kauai counties. At 1 p.m., the National Weather Service Doppler radar indicated an unexpected north-westerly shift in Hurricane Hannini, a major and extremely powerful storm. Hurricane Hannini is expected to make landfall at 11:30 tonight. This storm is projected to be a category five hurricane with winds up to 175 mph. Mandatory evacuation orders are currently in effect for all coastal areas in Hawaii, Maui, Kalawao, Honolulu, and Kauai counties. Please pack only necessary personal belongings, water, food, bedding, and medicines and head to your nearest evacuation shelter. Devastating damage and powerful storm surge with coastal flooding expected. During the storm, fire, police, and ambulance services will be unavailable. Do not venture outside."

The buzzes and chimes started over again as Auntie, Tad, and I stood around the radio in disbelief. Another bout of thrashing wind made it all real to us. We'd experienced island hurricanes before, Auntie most of all. I wondered whether she would heed the evacuation order and what it meant for our guests. Minutes passed as the alert cycled over and over again until Tad shut it off. Auntie stood there, almost statue-like, not saying a word.

"What's wrong?" I asked her.

A single tear slid down her cheek. "This is not how I expected it to end."

"What do you mean? There will be more guests."

She shook her head, chin still pointed toward the floor. For the first time in nearly a month, she appeared dejected, exhausted, and thin, like the last wisp of smoke on a dying candle.

"You know there won't. This is it. There's not enough time for tourists to start returning." She turned away and hobbled into her bedroom without saying another word. If storm preparations were going to be completed, Tad and I would have to see to them without her.

My first glimpse of Hurricane Hannini was an aerial view of the storm on Jim's laptop as he opened the door to their room after my incessant knocking. He was alone in the room. I could hear his girlfriend and her parents arguing through the wall.

"Still a category five?" I asked.

Jim glanced over his shoulder at me. "Yeah, with no sign of weakening. I've been called into the store for an emergency shift. Could you make sure Sarah and her family get to a shelter?"

"Of course. We'll bring them to the high school. You can meet us there afterward."

"Sorry for unloading them on you. Her parents can be... difficult."

A rap at the door behind me drew my attention. Sarah's father stood there, now dressed in slippers, shorts, and a Hawaiian shirt, and stunk of tropical-scented sunscreen, way too much of it caked all over his face and neck, as though he just squirted the lotion in his hand and slapped himself silly.

"The concierge, good. My wife and I were wondering if you could make reservations for us tonight somewhere good, perhaps one of those restaurants in town we passed on our way here."

I stared at Mr. Seren, unsure of how to respond. He knew about the hurricane warning, surely. Why was he acting so very touristy about it?

"I'm sorry, sir. You're aware a category five hurricane is going to hit the island tonight? We've all been ordered to evacuate."

"Nonsense. I just pulled up the weather. I'm from Florida, young man, and I know my hurricanes. This is going to miss us by at least twenty-five miles. It looks like you island people panic every time the wind blows."

"Even so, sir, here at the Estate Inn, our primary responsibility is the safety and well being of our guests. Right now, that means we will be evacuating your family to the local high school until the hurricane passes. Now we can't force you to evacuate. If you refuse, however, we will be obliged to cancel your reservation and ask that you vacate the premises."

Mr. Seren huffed at me. His cheeks turned a particular shade of red people experience when they don't get their way, like a lobster slowly boiling in a pot, hissing included.

"Sarah, get in here!" Mr. Seren called to his daughter in the next room. We were promptly joined by his wife, daughter, and son.

I felt surrounded and sulked back toward Jim. At this moment, my customer service skills were overburdened by my social anxiety. Thinking about the town hall meeting only days before, I didn't handle confrontation well at all, and it showed.

Mr. Seren turned to his daughter. "I thought you said this was a decent hotel. We would never be treated this way at a respectable facility."

I cleared my throat and mustered what remaining nerve I had. On an average day, the trade winds would cool me down enough to hide the beads of sweat collecting on my brow. But without them, and with the windows shut, the room became oppressive, sticky, and confining.

"I'm sorry, sir. Even the larger hotels will be heeding the evacuation orders. Come sunset, everyone on the coast will be at a shelter or further inland, at least fifty feet above sea level."

"Then I demand you find us another hotel that will accommodate us! I refuse to sleep on some cot in a high school gymnasium!"

I fretted even more. The tone in Mr. Seren's voice reminded me of Jeff and how he used to dominate everyone, me most of all. For the first time in a while, the scar on my scalp twinged. I felt like Harry Potter, and Mr. Seren was my Lord Voldemort. I wished someone would show up and sectum his sempra all the way to the emergency shelter.

Before a full panic attack could set in, my hero came to the rescue. Calder Wright, gym teacher extraordinaire. He picked up on my anxiety immediately. It didn't hurt that I was surrounded by four haoles in the midst of making an already tense situation intolerable.

"And who the hell is this?" Mr. Seren asked. "Not another lazy, inept employee? And where is the manager?"

Calder stepped in. "The owner, Alana Manalo, is downstairs packing what few possessions she can bring with her to the shelter. The rest of her belongings and this current building, her home, will remain behind, at risk of being destroyed. And I am Calder Wright, your friendly neighborhood evacuation assistant, here to *make sure* your family gets on your way before the storm arrives."

The tone of Calder's voice was indeed heroic. The way he emphasized "make sure" made sure Mr. Seren knew it wasn't a request. His confidence and his statuesque presence in the room forbade argument or debate. Mr. Seren shut up quite nicely. Within ten minutes, while I was still sitting on the bed with Jeff next to me, the Seren family, Sarah included, were out the door with the $1400 still in their pockets.

The financial loss wasn't Calder's fault at all. Guests like the Serens always seemed to find one way or another to not pay the full amount, either by leaving early or by stopping a credit card payment after the fact.

I heard their car peel out of the parking lot with Jim still sitting next to me. They had, without question, left him behind. "Sorry, dude."

"For what?" he asked. "This ain't on you. I expected Sarah to pull shit like this with her family over. Happened last time we went to Florida. They had me sleep on the floor in the den."

"Really?"

"Yeah, without an air mattress. Just me, a sheet and a pillow."

"But why? Why do you put up with that?"

"Look at me, Adam. Girls aren't exactly lining up to date me. I'm no one's idea of a good boyfriend. Or a good son-in-law. I ain't from a good family like you and Tad."

At that moment, Calder walked in. Jim tensed up. I read the signs quickly enough. He wasn't comfortable talking about this with Calder in the room, and I understood completely. If we had been talking about the worst aspects of my life, I wouldn't be comfortable with a stranger, either. And Jim and Calder, despite running in the same circles, didn't seem to know one another that well.

Jim wiped his eyes on his sleeve, attempting to hide his emotions from Calder, then collected his bag. "Anyhow, the store's waiting. I'll meet you at the shelter later on to help out."

Jim left the room, leaving Calder and me alone. I clicked a button on my phone to see the time. It was only 3 p.m. We had more than enough light left to board things up and make our way to the shelter.

Once downstairs, we joined Tad in the parking lot. A stiff wind dried the beads of sweat on my forehead, then moved inland to violently rustle the tufts of every palm tree in the way.

On the road, packs of shivering swimmers, pale as only mainlanders could be, fled the beach. I moved to the side of the house and peered through the bushes.

Waves crashed onto the beach, each one with a loud boom. I was surprised the storm surge started already, although I hadn't experienced a storm like this since I was a baby. Hurricanes occasionally struck Atlanta, sure, but they were always petering out by the time they did. Most of the time, storms in Atlanta only managed to flood some storm drains, leaving the rest of the city intact, quiet, and peaceful in an ominous "street sign is going to fly into your spleen" sort of way.

But this storm, Hurricane Hannini, seemed a behemoth, a torment with one purpose only, to drag the Hawaiian islands back into the sea.

I peered across the water at neighboring Lanai, the only other island visible from my current viewpoint. On a typical day, the view was tranquil, divine even. The island of Lanai beckoned to me across still waters, with the trade winds blowing against my back, enticing me to cross the calm waters and pay the island a visit. Lanai called to me like a good friend despite being separated by eight miles.

But now, with the storm surge and the Kona winds thrashing my face, Lanai seemed like a realm of monsters and demons trying their best to cross the divide and tear down everything good in my life. And beyond Lanai, darkening skies and ferocious waters. A category five. A Leviathan.

Calder stood behind me, his arm reaching around my shoulder, covering my chest, an intimate embrace I very much appreciated.

"Have you ever experienced a category five before?" I asked.

"Not like this. Never for every island. And before I got here, the radio said the storm is getting stronger."

"What are we going to do?"

With his long arm stretched around me, holding my other shoulder, he pulled me in tighter. "We're going to endure, then rebuild. It's all we can do, right? Maybe they're wrong. Maybe it won't be that bad."

"What about your family? Are they okay?"

"Yeah. They're already at Hana High, although they expect it won't be as bad that side of the island."

"You two done over there? Could use some help here!" Tad yelled over a strong gust of Kona winds, the winds responsible for changing the direction of the storm headed our way.

Calder let go of me and blushed. He seemed to have forgotten we had company. I peered inside to Auntie, a half-smile on her face as she spied on Calder and me. At that moment, I realized I was starting to heal, beginning to let Jeff go. I wondered what direction things would have headed without the storm. Curious, I questioned what would happen after, and said a silent prayer to whoever was listening that Lahaina, the Estate Inn, my home, would endure.

10

EVENING 19

After hours of boarding up windows, bringing in outdoor furniture, and moving Auntie's possessions from downstairs to upstairs, we packed our backpacks into Calder's truck to head to the high school on the opposite side of the highway, seventy-five feet above sea level.

Tad had left earlier to go to his own apartment and pack up some of his things. Living right along the highway, he happened to be in the mandatory evacuation zone and promised to join us after stopping by work. For some reason, violent winds meant he had to release and reel in every zipline, a five-person job on the best of days. And with the hurricane, only three people turned up.

Calder became edgier as the hours passed by. With the winds picking up and rain beginning to fall, I could tell he worried about his family. He kept checking his phone and shooting off random texts. Although Hana had a hurricane evacuation center, it was a smaller town with scant resources, and the high school was only twenty-five feet above sea level. A powerful storm surge could pose a risk, and flooding over Hana Highway and Honoapiilani Highway meant we were completely cut off from the rest of the island. There was even a ten-thousand foot high extinct volcano in the way.

We were among the first to arrive at the high school. Only 7 p.m., the sun had hardly begun to set. Being mid-July, folks were ill at ease with how early it was in hurricane season for a category five to hit the island. Those who were present hardly said a word to one another, their island spirit chased away by the prospect of impending doom.

Auntie spotted a friend of hers at a sign-in station who offered a free chair. I asked her if she needed help, but she waved me off, ordering me to find some way to be useful "for a change."

I knew she didn't mean to snap at me, but since we received news of the storm only a few hours before, she was not herself. I didn't blame her. When I had arrived, she had put on her hostess face, pretending everything was fine. But now her home was effectively lost. If not destroyed by the hurricane, this entire ordeal would prove the final nail in the coffin of her life plans.

Gone were the days of rum punch, apple bananas, empanadas, and a perpetual beachside holiday, a tropical dreamscape stolen away by the evil tax-man who now, ironically, provided shelter from the very storm that ruined it all.

"You okay?" Calder asked me as he led me further into the school. I looked around, realizing I would have attended this school if I hadn't been whisked off to the mainland.

"Who am I kidding?" I asked him. "Auntie, Tad, and I had no chance to raise the money to save the inn. Maybe the storm should destroy it. At least it'll save us the heartache of moving out."

"Come on. You don't mean that. No one wants to see you and Alana put out, especially me. But it's not your fault. It's not her fault, either. Shit happens."

"But she trusted me to help her save the inn. I feel like I'm letting her down, just like I let my mother down when I moved here."

I suddenly remembered my mother. It was almost midnight there. I wasn't sure if she knew about the hurricane. I hadn't heard a peep from her in days. As Calder tried to cheer me up again, I shot off a text message to her.

Mom, we're all fine. We're at Lahaina High riding out the storm. Love you. Call you later.

"-and it's not like you can control the weather. Maybe the clerk's office will grant you an extension because of the storm."

I looked up at Calder after pocketing my phone again. "Thank you for trying to cheer me up. I'm sorry for brooding. I'm just disappointed. Things finally started to go my way, and then this happened. It's a lot for me to take in."

As I leaned against a set of lockers in an empty, dark hallway and looked up at the taller Calder, I couldn't help but feel at ease. He didn't need to say anything to cheer me up. His gentle attention was enough. At that moment, I wanted him to kiss me. I could feel the tension building, the expectation of a shared first kiss.

If not for a woman yanking open the door from outside, sending a tepid and damp torrent through the hallway, a first kiss on the lips might have happened. The mood turned when it no longer became private.

"Come with me," Calder said as he grabbed my hand and led me deeper into the school. As we passed empty classrooms on our way away from the gymnasium where most folks checked in, I wondered where he was taking me.

On the far side of the school, around a bend and up a random flight of stairs, Calder opened a door into a well-maintained, garden-like greenhouse reserved for faculty.

Surrounded by plexiglass on all sides with a plexiglass ceiling, I was astounded by the view, perhaps the best in the entire town. Squinting through the rain-stained glass, I made out a raging ocean.

Hundreds of dancing palm trees swayed with each gust of wind. You could practically make out the gusts, as though they were powerful spirits playing a game of tug-of-war with one another for control of the island.

Behind us, the gentle slopes of Pu'u Kukui ascended into the clouds. The peak was hidden, as always, but everyone in Lahaina knew the sleeping volcano was there, occasionally bringing us much needed rain while providing us with crystal clear drinking water.

Below us, I saw the lights of the school project upward from one skylight or another as a steady stream of cars filed into the parking area, locals and tourists alike seeking shelter.

"Why did you bring me here?" I asked.

"Because this place is special to me. I fixed it up when I worked here. It became my own personal escape from the chaos below. I wanted to share it with you."

He moved in closer again, this time with nothing and no one around to interrupt. Placing his hands gently on my waist, he pulled me in until our hips pressed together. I braced myself as he moved in, my back firm against one of the windows. My hands, having a mind of their own, didn't know where to go. Dangling at my side, then waving around, they were eager for what was coming.

I held my breath, anticipating a heated first kiss. Calder did not keep me waiting. Removing one hand from my hip, he gently pulled at the back of my neck and leaned into me. I closed my eyes as our lips met in that first, strange and sensual caress. Lingering for just a second, our lips grazed until we both dove in, a fit of passion overtaking us.

He tasted of mint and honey as he first kissed my lower lip, sucking it a little, gently nibbling on it in a way that totally turned me on. He then moved to my upper lip, dampening it with his tongue, sending jolts of pleasure from my mouth to my brain.

The third kiss, the most sensual of them all, stunned me. I let out a single exhale as my heart skipped a beat. I had never been kissed like that before. He was sensual, passionate, tender, and commanding all at the same time.

Each gentle finger stroke on my neck and each nibble and twist of his mouth against mine made me quiver.

As he pulled away, the rain died down. The world became still, as though even the storm above us, and the wind spirits around us paused to say, "damn!"

And then the moment ended, almost as quickly as it began. The world became cold and dark after he pulled away. We both released a single chuckle. I imagined he was left dizzy, like me, from our brief connection.

"I'm sorry. Was that okay?" he asked.

I grinned, then used the back of my thumb to wipe saliva off my lower lip before chewing on it. "It was more than okay."

I suppressed my elation, stretched my legs, and arched my back to release some tension and discomfort in my pants, a tautness made worse by Calder's form-fitting jeans and a nearly-too-tight t-shirt that clung to his body from a bit of sweat and rain.

The moment was perfect, so perfect that I felt guilty—like I didn't deserve to be there. I recalled Jeff continually criticizing me, making me feel like I didn't deserve good things because I was useless, lazy, or stupid. In Jeff's own words, I was a "naïve, immature twink" who didn't deserve all the nice things he got for me. And by nice things, he always meant too-tight underwear, shirts, and pants he demanded I wear.

Evoking Jeff soured the mood, leaving the world grim and unfriendly. I became clammy and felt an urgent need to sit down.

Calder seemed to sense a change in my mood and looked confused. *I should tell him. He deserves to know how fucked up I am.*

"Everything okay?" he asked. He genuinely looked concerned, and reached out his hand, hanging onto my pinky in a playful "things are going to be fine" sort of way.

Calder led me to two folding chairs on the far side of the green-house. A single, empty cooler made up a sort of end table, littered with old magazines and yellow newspapers. I understood why Calder liked this place. It was like a little perch in the sky where one could see and think about the entire world, literally from a bird's-eye view.

Returning my attention to him, I tried to form the words to say, to reveal enough to make him understand without unloading so much that I might chase him away. He was flawlessly patient with me, and it sort of pissed me off. I searched for any kind of flaw in his personality, but my infatuation prevented me from seeing anything glaring. Unlike Jeff, Calder had no red flags as of yet.

"So…." I tried to say something but realized the filler word was a false start.

"Take your time." He sat in the chair opposite me, leaning forward with his elbows on his knees, twiddling his thumbs while looking at me, wholly and honestly looking at me. Not just toward me, but into my eyes.

I cleared my throat and broke eye contact with him. If I was going to do this, my brain told me I needed to look at the floor, the ceiling, the rain-soaked windows, anywhere but at him. The rough, patch-like fabric frayed under my fingers, giving my hands something to play with while I tried my best to use words.

"Before whatever this is between us continues." I paused. "And I very, very much want this to continue, I think you should know why I'm here. I'd like to tell you some stuff, but I don't want to answer any questions. Cool?"

"Cool," he said, shifting his stance, so he was leaning away from me a little more. I didn't know if he understood yet that the separation he created between us made things easier. If there was one thing I couldn't stand, it was being crowded. Jeff always invaded my space in a violent and intentionally controlling way, to the point where I felt any space I did have was leased to me by him.

I nodded at Calder and continued, "I didn't come to the island just to help Auntie. Back in Atlanta, I was in a horrible place. And by that, I mean a terrible relationship that wasn't good for me physically or emotionally. So all I've known when it comes to romance is that, and it's left me a little fucked up. I hope you understand. When I change or withdraw or freak out, it's because of that, not because of you."

There were a few moments of silence that, to me, felt like forever. Calder still had that gentle smile that was starting to grow on me.

"I'll understand if you want to run for the hills. You deserve more than someone as screwed up as I am."

He leaned forward again and placed his hands on mine, pulling them toward his mouth and kissing the back of my hands, a single soft kiss on each.

"How about you let me be the judge of what I do and don't deserve, huh? I don't care about your past. I'm interested in the man I see now. I think the Adam Frost I know now is pretty handsome, and amazing, and caring, and sensitive. And I want to know him more."

I blushed. I never considered myself very attractive. Only the women in my life ever called me that. "You think I'm handsome?"

"I thought I made that obvious the moment I first saw you."

"Yeah, but I like hearing you say it."

"Well, then, handsome man, how about we do what we said we would the other night. We take things slow, enjoy spending time with one another, and see where we end up? And if things ever become too much for you, promise me you'll let me know, and we can work through it. Sounds good?"

I smiled so much it ached. My cheeks had forgotten how to form and maintain an authentic look of glee.

Calder laughed, kissed my hand again, and helped me to my feet.

"I'll take that goofy grin as a yes. Now let's go find some dinner or something? I'm a growing boy and need to eat." He patted his belly three times, then took a last look outside. With the sun already below the horizon we could see close to nothing. The sky was a blanket of ominous clouds illuminated by the street lights from Lahaina. The wind menaced around with more force, and the rain began to pelt the windows. Despite the bulk of the hurricane still being a few hours offshore, the outer edge of it revealed our very long night ahead of us.

I held Calder's hand and squeezed, doing my best to wordlessly convey trepidation over what the next few days would bring, and how anxious waiting on the edge of a storm made me.

* * *

WITH THE GYMNASIUM NEARLY PACKED, FOLKS HAD TO SPILL INTO NEARBY classrooms just to find a place of their own. I lost track of Calder half an hour before, just as we had come downstairs and been spirited away as "strong young people" into various tasks.

My job was to work with Auntie in the cafeteria, preparing as much food as we could before the electricity went out. It seemed the school only had the generator hooked up to lights, outlets, and hot water in the gymnasium and locker rooms, meaning any food in the fridge needed cooking.

Auntie had me making as many sandwiches as possible from a

massive mound of deli meat donated from the local market and delivered by Jim. I felt terrible for the guy. He regaled me with the story of his getting kicked out of his tiny apartment because "there simply wasn't enough room for him," despite his paying all the rent.

And he mumbled about it non-stop. He let everyone with ears know how pissed he was and how, when this was all over, Sarah and he would "have words." We didn't hear the end of it until Auntie, fervently focusing on pots of rice and boiling pork, kicked him out of the kitchen.

A few minutes later, I got kicked out as well with a cart full of sandwiches. Despite all the chaos, nearly five-hundred people brought to the school, everyone was in good spirits and more or less behaved themselves.

Everyone behaved except the students who went to school there. They pranced around like they owned the place. To them, this was nothing more than one big, happy-go-lucky, co-ed sleepover. A group of parents in the middle of the gym argued about dividing them by gender to avoid all types of shenanigans.

Just as I reached the row of tables set up to dispense food, a powerful squall shook the roof. The beams stretching across the gym creaked, and the scoreboard they held in place vibrated, sending dust floating down onto the people below.

The lights flickered as I unloaded trays of sandwiches and took my place handing them out. Plate, sandwich, napkin, plate, sandwich, napkin. I did that fifty times in a row, passing out my meager helpings to locals and tourists. The tourists seemed to not play well with others. They all isolated themselves in the corner of the gym, trying their darnedest to secure better accommodations or tickets on non-existent flights off the island.

Another gust of wind beat against the roof and the lights went out for a few seconds, then flickered on and off a few times.

And when they came on for good, this time powered by the loud generator I could hear rumbling outside, I held out a plate with half a sandwich on it to my worst nightmare — a smirking Jeff Thatcher.

I dropped the plate and stepped back, pressed into the wall. A knot in my throat prevented me from releasing any sound whatsoever. No cry for help, no gasp, no exclamation. My eyes darted from one person to the next. No one paid any attention, every single person in the gym wholly unaware that while a hurricane was brewing outside, a calamity had befallen me in the very gymnasium that was supposed to be my shelter.

Jeff picked up the dropped sandwich and bit into it, taking his time to savor the moment. His eyes didn't move. They were transfixed on me as though he were a predator about to pounce on his prey.

He swallowed and used a napkin to methodically dab the corners of his mouth before rolling it into a ball and tossing it to the floor.

"It's good to see you, Adam. I can't tell you how relieved I am to find you here. You made me *very* worried." He obviously lied. And sounded more like a snake than I remembered.

Part of my brain didn't want to believe it was real, that there was no way he could have found me. I had a new phone, I never posted anything revealing on social media, and I even set up the fundraising page online in Tad's name, making sure no pictures of me were present.

And yet, here he was, trying to weasel his way back into my life, trying to assert control over me again.

"Why don't we go somewhere more private and... pick up where we left off?" Jeff asked, leaning toward me to whisper the last few words to hide from others his maniacal attitude.

I panicked. Pushing the table into him to create a gap in the row large enough for me to slip through, I barely managed to escape as he reached out to stop me.

Despite Jeff having a firm and painful grip on my wrist, I twisted my arm and freed myself before speed walking across the gym with only a few people in mind. I needed Auntie. Or Tad. Or Calder. Hell, I'd even settle for Jim at this point, but I couldn't find them.

Perhaps, in my haste, I didn't look hard enough. I eventually found myself in a dark hallway. The hairs on my neck stood on end as I felt a presence behind me. Spinning around, I saw Jeff waiting at the end of the hall, as though the two of us were playing a sadistic game of hide-and-seek. He was like the villain in a horror movie and, no matter how fast I moved, he would always be behind me. My voice disappeared. I couldn't call for help. Something about him prevented me from uttering any words.

The way he stood there, feet spread apart, arms slightly raised, head cocked to the side, made him seem demonic. And now, late at night enough for the hurricane to have reached nearly full-force, the deafening sound of rain made me freak out.

The scar on my scalp twinged, still tender after only three weeks of healing. And it reminded me of that night.

Three weeks ago, nearly to the day, I had come home after a double shift. I had taken the extra hours on a whim because, well, money.

And that meant by the time I got home, Jeff was waiting. And angry. And drunk.

My current feeling of nausea mounted as I remembered the argument we had in Atlanta over how stupid I was. I couldn't even remember to text him that I'd be late, and how he could do so much better than me. I didn't even manage to have dinner ready or laundry done.

I remembered apologizing to him until I was groveling because, at the time, I believed he was right, and I didn't want to lose him over my ineptitude. I was worthless. I was stupid. He did deserve more than me. And my groveling sent him into a rage.

Then that caricature of myself shattered when he first connected his curled fist with my stomach, sending me straight to the ground, followed by a swift and violent kick to my ribs, followed by a stomp on my head, his heel to my face. If he had been wearing shoes, I might have lost an eye.

And lastly, as I managed to raise myself to my hands and knees, the final assault. Jeff, in a fit of fury over my "ineptitude," grabbed me by the collar and started choking me with my own shirt.

I had thought then he would murder me, the way he laughed. He was having the time of his life as he tossed me around like a rag doll. The last thing I remembered on that fateful night weeks ago was the glass ashtray. I hung my head low as the heavy, shining object connected with my skull. And hours later, I awoke in the hospital, having been told I was found on the street blocks away from the apartment.

I honestly thought I escaped him when I came to Maui. But here he was, silently waiting for me to move, a puma ready to pounce.

The way he stood there terrified me the most. I feared this was it. Had he come here to finish what he started back in Atlanta?

The coward in me took over. I fled. The sound of our squeaking sneakers could be heard over the pounding rain. I knew he was chasing me. Even as I ran up one flight of stairs to the second level of the nearly empty school, with everyone enjoying the lighted gymnasium, I could tell he was gaining on me.

So I ran. Down another flight of stairs at the end of the second floor where I practically threw my body into a door's security bar. The change in pressure caused me to be sucked outside. After one strong gust of wind, the door slammed shut behind me.

I continued to run, the wind tossing me around like a feather. I dashed further away from the school as the razor-blade like rain stung my skin until I found myself at the baseball diamond.

I didn't know if Jeff had followed me outside. I didn't care. Without looking back, I was through an empty gate and took shelter in one of the dugouts, water already pooling below me, filling the small structure too quickly for it to drain away.

I crouched on the bench as the storm enveloped me, screaming in my ear as though it were a dark spirit intent on driving me insane.

But at least I was protected from most of the rain. And after a few minutes, I knew Jeff hadn't followed me outside.

I should call for help was a singular thought I couldn't act on. I pulled my phone out. No signal. With nowhere to go, I buried my head between my knees and rocked back and forth on the metal bench, where I started to have a complete meltdown.

11

MORNING 20

I<small>T WAS PAST MIDNIGHT, AND NOTHING HAD CHANGED.</small> I <small>FELT LIKE A STATUE</small> in a graveyard, curled into a protective ball as the storm raged around me. It inhaled and exhaled against me with a breath that felt tepid, clammy, and sinister.

I had been through hurricanes before, but this one took the cake. It wasn't just a hurricane. It was a titan, the pent up and released rage of some forgotten ocean god.

Just as I thought the hurricane was unrelenting, it seemed to calm, if only for a moment. The break made me wonder whether I was in the eye of the storm, although it was much too early for that. I heard on the radio as I prepared dinner that the eye would pass over Maui six hours from now.

I lifted my head up. Cheeks raw from the mixture of salty wind and even saltier tears, I squinted through the rain, now falling straight from the sky as though God had turned on a faucet.

And I saw her. A girl standing on the pitcher's mound. I rubbed my eyes, thinking I imagined her, but she was still there, standing upright and proud and untouched by the storm, with sadness and grief written on her face.

Am I dead? Did Jeff actually get me?

I admired the young woman, with her thick black hair that flowed calmly down her back. She wore the most amazing red dress that swirled around her, barely disturbed by the wind. She had a single pink lily tucked behind her ear. She seemed to glow with an aura that stopped the rain around her from reaching the ground.

In her hands, she held a feather fan. I recognized it as a Kahili, often shown in portraits of Hawaiian royalty. It was also just as undisturbed by the hurricane, dry as a bone.

"Who are you?" I asked. My mousy, cracking voice was captured by the hurricane, so it was unlikely she heard.

She smiled at me, and I felt all my panic and anxiety melt away. I looked at the young woman and knew then that I was going to be okay.

She raised her free hand and gestured toward the school. I understood instinctively that it was safe to return. When I looked toward the building, then back to her, she vanished. The storm began to pick up, and I knew I had to get back inside. The dugout did not a hurricane shelter make.

I worked my way around the building toward the entrance by the gymnasium. Even after midnight, some people were still arriving, most likely holdouts who thought they didn't need to evacuate away from the shore.

I followed one such group in, a pair of tourists by the look of them, and crept around them into the gym.

The lights were dimmed. Over a hundred cots were laid out, occupied by mounds of people trying to fall asleep, only to be awakened by a loud snort, snore, or roof rattle whenever the storm picked up.

The roar of the rain against the gym's metal roof proved too deafening for many. Nearly every other cot was aglow with harsh blue light from a phone or tablet.

As I walked between the rows of bodies, I did my best to carefully observe each person, afraid I might stumble upon Jeff again.

Once through the gym, I heard some laughter coming from the hallway. Following it, I found Auntie in a classroom, desks pushed together to form a table where she was playing poker with some friends.

Tad and Jim had their own game going in the corner and laughed and jested with one another as they played at war, slapping the pile of cards to declare victory each round.

They were the first two to spot me shivering in the doorway. Tad shot to his feet and flew across the room at a speed that belied his size.

He caught me just as my knees gave out. My mind didn't realize how exhausted my body was. I awoke hours later, the storm still raging, my shirt, pants, socks, and shoes removed, drip-drying over the back of a nearby chair.

I peeked over the sleeping bag I found myself tucked into and spotted Tad's hulking figure leaning against the closed door. When he noticed I was awake, he glared at me and raised his finger to his mouth to demand my silence.

I sat up, shivering as the sleeping bag slid down my torso. The room was unexpectedly cold.

Staggering to my feet, wrapping the sleeping bag around my shoulders, I shuffled to the window, mindful of some of the other bodies littered around the room, which I now realized was a teacher's lounge. Some of the older evacuees, including Auntie, claimed the small number of couches out of both necessity and comfort.

Auntie, despite having the disposition of a young woman, was still seventy-five. Her days of sleeping on cold floors were long behind her.

I looked at some of the others on the floor, their faces lit up only by the menacing, gray glow of the sun trying to penetrate the torment swirling above our heads. I found Jim, snoring in a corner, but no sign of Calder or anyone else I recognized.

I finally reached the window and gasped at the sight of naked palm trees bending in the wind, like toothpicks ready to snap.

Some cars in the parking lot had slipped against the force of the wind. A few tipped onto their side. I placed my hand on the window, relieved to realize they were hurricane resistant glass, and could undoubtedly withstand the beating.

As a single tear slid down my cheek at the sight of my new, old home being torn to shreds, a heavy hand landed on my shoulder, causing me to jump. Half expecting Jeff, I could breathe again when I saw Tad standing next to me, silently beckoning me to follow him outside.

As he led me through the lounge, I noticed the clock on the wall that read 5 a.m. We would be only a handful of people awake at this hour. Through the gymnasium and into the locker room, Tad spun the dial on one of the padlocks and pulled out our bags, tossing me a dry shirt and shorts, and a pair of spare slippers I packed.

As I slipped the shirt over my head, I could still feel him glaring at me, angry that I had disappeared for so long, ventured out into the storm, and came back a complete mess.

I wondered if telling him about Jeff would make things easier or harder. Now clothed, I sat down on a bench across from Tad, who seemed to expect me to start first.

"How much do you know about why I moved here? How much did my mom tell you two?"

Tad raised his arms and curled his fists, waving them in the air to express his anger. "And what does that have to do with you going for a midnight stroll during a hurricane? Auntie almost passed out worried!"

"Just answer the question, please."

My eyes began to well up, something Tad didn't fail to notice. He sat down, never failing to keep eye contact with me. I could tell he was still frustrated, but he raised his eyebrows, cranked his head, and rubbed the back of his neck.

"She didn't say much. Just that your boyfriend attacked you, and you came here to get away from him. Why?"

I hesitated, never having spoken to anyone aside from Calder about this. Even Calder didn't get the brunt of the details. I unloaded on Tad in a monologue of word garbage, as though the last five years of my life demanded release.

"It started off with small things, you know? Putting me down, yelling about little things, getting drunk, and grabbing my wrists too tight. Then he drank more. And got angrier. He would punch walls and throw shit, and then he decided he was tired of fixing the holes and started to hit me instead.

"First, pushing me down, telling me how useless and worthless I was. Then slapping my arms and back to leave giant welts. Twisting my arm so hard it still hurts sometimes. Not to mention becoming more forceful and violent in bed."

Tad squirmed a little. I could tell he wasn't too keen on talking about sex, despite how gay-friendly he turned out to be.

I cleared my throat and wiped a forming tear before it could fall. Too much water was falling already from the storm. Now wasn't the time for crying. Tad started to say something, but I stopped him.

"Please. I just want to finish this. I need to get this off my chest."

He stopped himself, and gestured for me to continue, but shifted over to the bench to sit next to me. I could tell he struggled with how to handle this, and the way he turned into me to listen seemed to be the best way he could show he cared.

"I knew I had to escape. I suppose the moment I decided to happened a few months before I actually left. I had a friend, Debbie, in a similar situation. Her husband was just as violent. The two of us had planned to escape together, to come here together. But then her husband killed her, and then himself. I never told anyone that, even Mom. Even when I disappeared for a few days to go to her funeral, no one knew, but when I came back, Jeff was even worse."

I looked up at a skylight in the locker room ceiling. The sky turned bright as we entered the eye of the hurricane. The wind died. The rain stopped. For a moment, I saw a bright white wall of clouds passing overhead. Everything went eerily silent.

"I lost my ambition to leave when she died. We weren't particularly close. She was in a guild in an online game we played together. I didn't even know her address. Jeff never let me have real friends.

"But then that night came three weeks ago. Jeff was drunker than usual and decided to take out all his rage on me. He didn't just attack me. He...."

I paused, swallowing a wall in my throat that held back a tsunami of wails and sobs and uncontrollable grief and anxiety. Breathing in and out didn't seem to stop what was coming. I knew all too well the warning signs of an impending panic attack.

It took Tad's firm, steady hand on my shoulder to pull me away from it. The shock of his warm hand on my cold, clammy skin was enough to settle me and allow me to continue.

"He was brutal. He didn't just attack me. He tried to kill me. Sometimes I wake up at night panicked, still feeling him strangling me with my own shirt. And then he dragged me to the street and tossed me to the curb, like gutter trash.

"I don't think he meant for me to survive. When I woke up in the hospital, I remembered Debbie. After feeling the same fear she did before she died, I knew I didn't want to become her, so I ran away."

"Brah...." Tad was at a loss for words. I could tell. His hand around my shoulder turned into an arm wrapped around my back. I leaned into him and felt, in a way, that Tad became more a brother to me than a cousin. Still, though, I felt guilty for unloading this all on him when who I really needed were the police, and a whole army of therapists I couldn't afford.

I enjoyed the familial moment for a minute, the two of us sitting in silence save the clattering coming from the other side of the locker room, sounds of people starting to wake up.

"That's not the worst of it, though. You want to know why I went outside, why I disappeared for hours?"

Tad nodded, losing his grip on me as I stood up and paced back and forth in a panic.

"He's here," I mumbled, before stopping and turning toward him. "Jeff's here, on Maui. He came up to me while I was serving food. I freaked and ran outside and hid in the dugout for a few hours until..." I hesitated, not sure whether to tell Tad about the mysterious woman I saw. It would confuse him just as much as me.

Tad shot up to join me. His anger mounted, this time not at me. He puffed his chest up and curled his fists. "You say he's here? In the building?"

"Doubtful. Jeff wouldn't stick around. I still have the police report, and there are some cops here, right?" Fueled by Tad's anger, I did something totally out of character and punched the locker with my palm. It definitely hurt me more than the locker. "I only hope he died in the storm. Knowing my luck, though, he's fine. I just know he came here to finish what he started. This time there's no doubt. He looked and acted like he wanted to murder me for leaving him."

I spent the next few minutes talking Tad down. He pretended at vigilantism, as though he alone would hunt Jeff down and kill him for daring to attack his family. But Jeff was gone. I knew this. Without knowing why, the woman in the storm seemed to want to protect me, whoever she was.

Tad and I left the locker room after fetching the report, the only proof I could offer to local police.

The lights in the gym were turned on now. People started waking up, a few of them going just outside the gym to assess the damage around the school before the storm picked up again.

A lonely policewoman yelled at them to get back inside, knowing the calm would only last a few more minutes before the eye passed, this time with more force than the front side of it.

Tad tried to get her attention, but it wasn't until she had everyone safely back inside that she paid us any mind. The sky already started to darken, and the roar of the wind resumed, as though the very same, angry ocean god I imagined with Calder flipped a switch.

The whole room grew quiet when a wall of rain struck the school, shaking the rafters above. I heard one idiot, a mainlander, warning people that the roof couldn't take much more, as though he were an expert in hurricane-resistant design.

Wanting more privacy, Tad led the policewoman, Officer Lanna, as she introduced herself, into a nearby empty classroom.

I explained the situation as she read over the police report. All it took was one look at me to know it was real. I still sported slight bruising under my eye even twenty days later. I wondered if the bruise would ever fade completely.

The way she spoke gave me hope. I thought of the mysterious woman and imagined that if she had a voice, it would sound like Officer Lanna. They even looked similar, with their dark, tanned skin, long hair, and small, albeit sturdy frame, only Officer Lanna wore her dark blue police uniform with black shoes and black utility belt, rather than a magnificent pink and red dress.

Tad, meanwhile, stood in the doorway, making sure no one came in to disturb us.

"I understand you're frightened. Are you sure he's not still here?"

I shrugged. "When I came back inside, I looked around. I'm pretty sure he left."

She continued to review the police report, focusing intently on Jeff's picture. "If you're certain, I'll notify the staff at the front door to let them know to detain him should he return. I'll also tell the other officers. And when this storm is over, I want to see you first thing at the station to file a report. We'll need to get a protection order. For now, that's all we can do."

"What? Can't you arrest him? He tried to murder me! Twice!"

"I can call the Atlanta PD once the phone lines are up to see what our options are. But unless he has an arrest warrant in Georgia, there's little we can do. I understand you're frustrated. I need you to trust me when I say I will help you. In the meantime, I'd suggest you spend as little time alone as possible. And I promise to get more police patrols around your work and home."

I buried my face in my hands. I wanted to scream into them but held back. It wasn't Officer Lanna's fault. She was a police officer. She had to follow the letter of the law. I just wanted this all to end, for Jeff to rot in a jail cell on the other side of the country. I needed Maui, now tainted by his presence, to be my Maui again.

I looked out the window at more stripped palm trees and realized that after this storm, it would take a long time before things felt normal. Jeff was only one small part of all of my stress. The inn, Auntie's health, my father, and even my blossoming relationship with Calder combined like a weight on my chest. I could only manage, at best, shallow breaths, and felt my heart racing a mile a minute.

The lights in the hallway flickered a few times, then went cold. I heard audible gasps and screams from the gymnasium. Officer Lanna sprang to her feet, her professional instincts taking over, but stopped before she left the room.

"Are you going to be okay? You look pale. A social worker friend of mine is here. You want to talk to her?"

I waved her off, not wanting to burden her more than she already was, and recalled a social worker who talked to me in the hospital who only made things worse, suggesting the best way to handle the situation was to press charges and face Jeff in a courtroom. I shivered at the thought of taking the witness stand with him seated across from me. I wasn't strong enough. Yet.

Morning turned into quite a melancholy afternoon. For most of it, Tad decided to keep me under lock and key until he and Jim searched the entire building for any sign of Jeff.

I resigned myself to lying in a corner on one of the many couches, my head resting on Auntie's lap while she stroked my hairline and hummed, poorly, some of her favorite songs, the way my mother used to when I was younger.

I imagined, for a moment, that Auntie, much older than Mom, did this for her, just as Auntie's mother or father did for them.

Her humming, a swig of rum from her hidden flask, and the melodic thrashing of the rain against the sturdy windows made me almost fall asleep. Almost.

But periodically, my brain decided to flash the haunting image of Jeff in the dark hallway above, him chasing me down like I was a camp counselor to his Jason Voorhees. My whole body would shudder. Auntie would calm me down, then restart her current tune.

I got fed up. I didn't want to just lie around all day while everyone was occupied around me, and every time some otter-like white guy walked by the door of the teacher's lounge, I got nervous thinking it was Jeff.

I needed to do something.

"Where's Calder been?" I asked Auntie.

She stopped humming for a moment. "I think he set up a campsite of sorts in the cafeteria for the children. He's most likely been there all night."

As I got up to leave, Auntie scolded me. Even she seemed to want to limit my movements.

"Auntie, come on. There's literally twenty people in the hallway, and the cafeteria is only a few doors down."

She scoffed, then leaned back and resumed her humming. I questioned her sanity for a moment, as I swore I saw her still stroking my not-present hairline, only to realize she was conducting to her own personal orchestra.

I didn't know how anxious she was over the state of the inn and swore silently to myself to make sure she would be all right after the storm ended.

Moments later, I stood in the doorway to the cafeteria to a sight to behold, a happy one that shooed my melancholy away.

Calder was being chased by a chain of arm-linked children, a tired-looking Jim in the middle, playing a raucous round of blob tag in a space way too small for the game.

I watched as Calder ran into a corner, now pinned in by a line of children, a faux look of horror on his face. He seemed to be the sort of guy who made an excellent gym teacher. His style with the children became more animated and lively compared to the Calder I had met in a town hall parking lot.

His smile faded when he spotted me by the door, but only for an instant. The teacher in him took over as the kids broke formation and pounced on him, laughing and giggling until he managed to blow on his whistle and end the game.

He looked at his watch and ordered the kids to return to their parents, now nearly dinner time.

The kids all whined about wanting to continue, but Jim stepped in and helped usher them out of the cafeteria, leaving Calder to clean up whatever mess they had left.

On his hands and knees, he got to collecting hand-drawn pictures strewn about, drawings of the kids, their homes, and their stick-figure families.

"I heard what happened," he said as I knelt down to help. "Are you okay?"

As we both reached for the same drawing, his hand found its place on mine. I felt him trace his thumb around my knuckle. Compared to his warmth, I could tell I was cold and clammy. I just wanted to go home, to fall asleep in my beach-side apartment, and wake up to the sound of a calming ocean.

Most of all, I wanted to not think about Jeff.

"I don't know how to be," I whispered to him.

Calder didn't press me any further. Instead, we spent time together cleaning up the cafeteria. It felt good to be alone with him, and I found myself not wanting this tranquil moment to end.

12

AFTERNOON 22

ONCE THE STORM ENDED, IT TOOK ANOTHER DAY BEFORE THE ROADS WERE cleared enough to return to Lahaina, and we were given the okay to leave by Officer Lanna. I squished myself into the middle of Calder's truck with Auntie to my right. We were both shivering from a chill in the air left in the hurricane's wake.

Auntie took my hand. I could tell she was weak by the way she clung to me, shuffling her feet as though her legs were too heavy to move.

I could sense her apprehension. Like me, she worried about her home. News of the inn hadn't reached us amidst other more pressing topics. In particular, all of the major hotels on the island were closed, their doors still locked and covered by metal sheeting.

What triggered most people at the school was the indefinite closure of the airport. The fuel tanks had been compromised by the storm. Until they were emptied, repaired, and refilled by way of multiple fuel planes from the mainland, everyone was stuck.

We also knew that both roads to Hana were closed until trees could be cleared. With cell towers down and electricity out, Calder had no way to contact his family. Even now, he tried to reach them on his phone, but his calls kept failing. Frustrated, he kicked the side of his truck before climbing in.

"I'm sure they're fine," I said to him.

He breathed out his tension and his jaw relaxed, although his knuckles were still white from gripping the steering wheel. "I know. That side of the island didn't get hit as hard. You mind if I stay with you for a few more days until I can find somewhere else to go?"

"Of course. Stay as long as you need. As long as the inn is still standing..."

Before he could thank me, we were surprised by the whole truck dropping a few inches. I turned around to see Tad and Jim hopping into the truck bed. Tad banged on the side, eager to go, and we pulled out of the still-full parking lot, through a sea of tourists doing their best to secure a way off the island.

I didn't want to let on to Auntie or Calder that I was checking the faces of every single one of them, hoping not to find Jeff. In truth, I hoped he didn't get to another shelter. I wanted nothing more than to read a report of his demise in the newspaper.

I could only be so lucky.

What should have been a ten-minute drive took forty minutes — forty minutes of Auntie clutching my hand while dabbing tears from her eyes with a spare hankie.

We passed the market, the parking lot empty aside from some over-turned carts and fallen palm trees. As we entered Lahaina, the city seemed wounded. I wondered if the magnificent banyan tree in the heart of town endured, although I hoped it had weathered too many storms to suffer any lasting damage.

The tension in the cab stifled me. Despite the windows being rolled down to let the 65-degree air in, it felt hard to breathe. As we rounded the corner toward the inn, I let go of Auntie's hand and wrapped my arm around her, prepared to comfort her for the worst.

But the tension vanished the instant our magnificent white palace came into view. Hopping the curb to work around a fallen palm tree, we pulled into the parking lot.

Auntie jumped up and down in her seat, her palms striking the roof of the truck, excited.

"Oh! Tad! Adam! It's still here! My home is still here!"

I had never seen the woman so happy. Even Calder, brooding over his family, tooted the horn in celebration as we pulled up to the front steps.

Moments later, I stood on the front steps, my jaw agape.

Looking over at our neighbors, a single-family residence, I gasped. It seemed their house didn't meet a flying tree it didn't let inside. Their roof was ripped completely off, while ours, at least from the front, was unscathed.

While Auntie and Tad went inside, Calder and Jim followed me to the back of the house. The sand felt squishy, still waterlogged from storm surge. Jim lent me his phone, mine still dead, so I could shine it into the crawlspace below the house. Aside from some standing water, I saw no sign of damage.

And once in the backyard, our sheer luck became obvious. Aside from some pieces of lawn furniture that didn't belong to us strewn across the yard, and the fence surrounding the property gone, blown from the posts, there was zero evidence of any significant damage.

I inhaled the scent from the beach. It smelled rotten, of refuse and seaweed mixed, left to bake in the sun. I walked the path up the dune to the beach.

The ocean looked like absolute carnage, still churning more than usual. It seemed the only lasting consequence was two feet less of beach space outside the inn.

I breathed a giant sigh of relief and returned to the inn to sounds of Auntie squealing with delight, forgetting momentarily the tax burden she still bore.

She waved her cane at us as we walked into the kitchen from the back door. "Roll up your sleeves, boys! There's work to do!"

"What's the rush?" I asked. "It's not like we have any guests."

"You go dumb, Makani? The island's full of them and all the big hotels are closed up!"

I was shocked by her suggestion. For her entire career, Auntie never let a person in need pay to stay at her inn, but now she was jumping for joy at the idea of taking advantage of tourists trapped here.

"You're not saying we gouge them, are you?" I asked.

"Rubbish! We'll charge them a fair rate. Why shouldn't we?" She hobbled across the room and flung open the pantry to reveal a fully stocked closet, unspoiled by the storm. Considering it had only been two days of cold temperatures, and how dry the pantry remained, even the fruits and vegetables were still good to go. Auntie launched into action.

"We have a full larder, we have a stocked bar, and we have plenty of rooms to spare! Calder, will you be a dear and get the jugs of water from my bedroom? I filled them before we left. And Tad, sweetie, go back to the school and start collecting some guests. We have twelve guest rooms to fill, $120 a night, cash only! Yes. That's a nice, round number!"

Tad chuckled. He knew better than to argue with Auntie. He elbowed me in the ribs to get my attention, leaned in, and whispered to me, "Don't let her get too riled up. She hasn't slept in two days."

Auntie heard him, and balked at him, throwing a roll of paper towels across the room with a force that belied her age, striking Tad in the head. "Why are you still here? Go! Get me some paying guests!"

Tad backed out of the room, glaring at Auntie in a playful, loving way. That left just Jim and me.

"Makani, dear." She hobbled across the room before stopping in front of Jim, seeming to notice him standing there for the first time. "Jim, what are you still doing here? Don't you have things to do?"

"I'd rather not," he mumbled.

Auntie shrugged. "Fine. Just make yourself useful. Go clean up the outside. Find my patio furniture if you can. I'm sure it couldn't have gone far. Maybe check the neighbor's living room!" She let out a loud belly laugh.

"Auntie! What a thing to say!" Still. I couldn't help but laugh with her. It was a relief to see her so alive, so full of hope, and I knew the house next to us sat vacant most of the year anyhow. Chances were the owners wouldn't show up for weeks to assess the damage. That or they'd pay some property management firm to take care of it for them.

She playfully slapped my cheek as Jim left the room, leaving just the two of us, then turned on a dime and became very serious.

"Do you need me to go to the police with you?" she asked.

I knew immediately that Tad told her about our conversation with Officer Lanna, and considering we saw her only minutes before at the school, it was too early for me to go to the station to file a report. I shook my head.

"Fine, but promise me you'll go nowhere alone!"

I huffed and mumbled a yes back to her, but she gripped my chin between her thumb and index finger.

"I mean it, Adam. I saw how scared you were of that man. If you step one foot off this property without Calder or Tad with you, I'll put you on the first flight off this island. I won't have you risk your life by going for a stroll."

"I promise."

She rubbed my chin where she had pinched me. "Good. And when you go to the station, I'm going with you. I want to hear everything the police say. I won't let them brush you aside because they think you're some haole.

"You came here to be safe, so safe you'll be. The day that bastard lays another finger on you is the day I go to prison for murder. I'll show him for hurting one of my boys!"

I sniffled and blinked my eyes as they began to water. Auntie had a way of warming my heart. Coming to Maui suddenly seemed the right choice for me, after all.

I hoped when this was all over, if we were able to save the inn, I could bring my mother and sister out here for good. I wondered for a moment if they would come.

That led me to think about saving the inn. The news said the airport would be down for a week, at least. If we managed to fill every room to capacity, at $20 a day cost per person, that meant only $6,000 in profit. We still had a few weeks to find $20,000 more to pay the tax bill.

In those three weeks, I could earn perhaps another $800 from the market, but that would almost certainly go toward expenses for the inn.

We needed money, and we needed it fast, and without the internet or electricity for the foreseeable future, I couldn't check my fundraising page. And now was the perfect time to try to make it go viral. Folks from the mainland would be pouring money in left and right to support us.

As I helped Auntie prepare for our guests by checking every room, everything came rushing back to me. When I was with people, I could distract myself. But alone in empty hotel rooms with nothing but my own thoughts, my mind jumped from worrying about the inn to worrying about Jeff. Back and forth like a sadistic game of neurotic pong.

And then I heard music coming from downstairs, albeit music intermixed with a fair amount of static.

At least Auntie's radio works. That's something.

I heard the sound of tires on gravel coming from the front. I exited the last guest room, beds made, bathrooms scrubbed, and pillows fluffed. I thought about leaving our care package for the guests with complimentary water, treats, and information on local venues, an idea I implemented two weeks ago when I could do nothing but sit at a table, but decided against it.

If we were to make this work, we needed to make sure we didn't waste things like potable water or foodstuff. With snacks and water, guests were more likely to lock themselves in their rooms all day instead of having a pleasant experience with Auntie downstairs.

We needed these environmental refugees to go back to the mainland and tell others about the "port in the storm" the Estate Inn became.

I pulled the curtain back on one of the front windows to see Tad's truck popping and creaking as he pulled into the parking lot, a line of cars behind him.

"One, two….. ten, eleven, twelve, thirteen, fourteen," I counted.

My grin matched Tad's as he climbed out of the truck and noticed me. He waved, then directed the cars in, orchestrating them so they would all fit in our nearly too-tiny parking lot.

He then ran to the back corner, where I noticed Jim working on putting up our fallen basketball hoop. Tad grabbed a ball from the ground and tossed it across the parking lot, to be caught by a young boy, likely ten or eleven. Within seconds, four more boys and girls joined in while their parents went inside.

As I went to help Auntie greet the guests, I realized the door to my bedroom was open, the drapes covering my ocean-facing windows flapping in the wind. I wondered if we had overlooked some damage, but there was no sign on the floor of broken glass or debris, and the carpet wasn't wet.

I crept into the room, my body stiff and edgy, pleading to myself that Jeff hadn't crashed here, hadn't managed to infiltrate the inner-most sanctum that was my bedroom.

Would he be this bold?

Water ran in the bathroom, the door opened only a crack. There was no electricity, no hot water, and no steam. I thought it might be Calder, taking an ice-cold shower after working around the inn.

Not one to take a chance, I grabbed a lonely baseball bat by the door with a tag attached to it that read, "Just in case, -T."

When did Tad put this here?

With the baseball bat in hand, prepared to do the same thing to Jeff that he did to me with a glass ashtray, I raised it above my head and yanked the door open to find a shivering Calder cleaning himself quickly, to avoid staying under the frigid water for too long.

He jumped when I yanked the door open, and instinctively covered his bits with his hand before breathing a sigh of relief after realizing it was me.

I decided Jeff wasn't so bold as to camp in my room. Calder, however, was undoubtedly far from meek. After getting over being startled, he no longer covered himself, revealing the full sight of him. I blushed but continued checking him out anyhow.

Like a giddy gay boy in a bathhouse, I couldn't help but admire a view I most definitely liked. Even while bathing in cold water, he was packing.

"I don't know how long the water will last. Care to join me?"

I hesitated, then took a sniff of myself. So occupied with Jeff at the school, I realized I hadn't showered since before the storm. My clothes were dank. The promise of even a cold shower with Calder seemed a treat.

I closed and bolted my door just as the first wave of guests made their way upstairs, and tossed my dirty clothes in the bin.

While Calder didn't have a shy bone in his body, I did. I walked in the bathroom, cupping my hands over my junk, and modestly stepped in, facing away from him.

I felt his slippery hand on my shoulder, then shivered as he took a small sand pail filled with water and poured it over my head.

Gasping and wiping the water from my eyes, I felt him spin me around. When I opened my eyes again, he was looking down and biting his lower lip. It seemed he was just as pleased with me as I was with him, although I didn't know why.

Calder had six inches on me in height, with broad, built shoulders and a physique that spoke truth to his fitness and virility.

I was lanky and thin, with a thick scruff covering my entire face, the rough scruff I inherited from my father. Most of all, I was so without muscle and nearly hairless everywhere else that, if not for the ability to grow a beard, one would think puberty had almost skipped me.

Looking down at Calder and me, compared side by side, now half erect, I couldn't help but feel inept, a sentiment Jeff liked to amplify above all else.

But Calder was the exact opposite. With his soapy hands, he prepared to rub me down but stopped just an inch from my skin.

"May I?" he asked gently. The fact that he asked for permission opened me up.

As I continued to stare at him, now having mostly adjusted to the water, I nodded, and he got to work. His soapy hands massaged every bit of me, starting with my shoulders and neck, then down my back, around to my front. I giggled as he rubbed under my armpits.

He traced his thumbs around my nipples, both erect from the icy water. I shuddered as he focused on them more. Jolts of pleasure caused my back to arch involuntarily with every swirl.

He lathered his hands again, working his way down, and down, and down, skipping over my now full erection. Kneeling so that the water cascaded over him completely, he massaged his soapy hands between my legs, then down my thighs, calves, and the tops of my feet.

I struggled as he worked between my toes, mindfully cleaning every inch of me.

With fresh lather, he went right for the prize. As his surprisingly warm hands worked up and down, I buckled back, gripping the sides of the shower. He stood up, wrapping his arm around my back and firmly grabbing my ass, pulling me toward him.

Releasing one hand, I wiped some suds from my chest and grabbed him as well, sizing up his sevenish inches as we worked on one another, stroking and tugging. As the heat between us built, I took the initiative, and leaned in, locking my lips to his.

They remained fixed, fused together by passion. Staggering backward, I accidentally turned off the water. We continued to slide our hands back and forth in unison, our legs quivering at the same time as I felt the urgency of release rising.

"I'm getting close," I mumbled, our lips still pressed together.

"Me too!" He pulled at me even faster. I tightened my grip and did the same, until we both seized simultaneously, covering our hands and bellies. The moment lasted longer than I had expected, both of us doing our best to hold the other up as we trembled and quivered, our hips bucking with every ecstatic pulse.

And then it ended. Our lips separated, and we both let out a single chuckle.

"That was," I said.

"Yeah…"

He released his hand from my ass and slid it up my back, pulling me into him as I wrapped my arms around his burly, furry torso. We lingered for a few minutes until our joint high wore off, then cleaned ourselves off again, drying off, and lying down, still naked, on my bed, staring up at the ceiling as a gentle breeze blew through the room.

I noticed the temperature had risen since we arrived at the inn. No longer a chilly sixty-five with an ice-cold wind, I felt as though the trade winds had reasserted themselves. The island seemed to come to life again, with the sun shining, birds chirping, and sounds of laughter floating in from downstairs. Maui was damaged, sure, but he would soon be right again. Just like his people, Maui was resilient and hardy.

I began to feel similar hardiness in myself. With Calder lying next to me, our arms and legs entwined, I knew that the people in my life wouldn't let me down. Maui wouldn't let me down.

I closed my eyes and pictured the woman in red standing on the pitcher's mound, powerful enough to stop the rain, and knew, somehow, the island was watching out for me. So were Tad and Auntie. And now, Calder. I dozed off, awash in optimism. Everything was going to be okay.

13

MORNING 26

Auntie couldn't help but doze off in the chair next to me despite the flurry of activity in the police station, whereas I was nearly blinded by the bright fluorescent lights at seven in the morning.

Three days had passed since we packed our inn so full of guests, many of whom insisted they pay a higher rate for their rooms. Some offered upward of $200 a night due to them unexpectedly having the time of their lives. They set up a tip jar that needed emptying multiple times a day. When the hurricane hit, they thought their vacation ruined, but we transformed that negative experience into an "off-the-grid style vacation extravaganza."

Tad took them out on island excursions as best he could, showing the families with children what fruits and vegetables were safe to eat, collecting them to bring back to the inn to supplement Auntie's diminished pantry. He found so many coconuts.

Every night we managed to feed our guests rice and taro, coconut, papaya, and cooked breadfruit. We even had dried meats from emergency supplies our guests picked up at the enduring, vibrant Banyan tree in the heart of Lahaina, hardly damaged by the storm thanks to large wires securing most limbs. Auntie, Calder, and I were amazed at the bounty Tad acquired, wondering how every fruit hadn't managed to be blown down by the storm. I admired my cousin, a bastion of local knowledge, learned from identifying every fruit tree and edible plant on his zipline course.

He had to do something productive, he said. It would be weeks before his company opened the lines again. Jim, meanwhile, spent most of his time at the inn or the market, spending nights in my old bedroom. He brooded mostly over having broken up with his girl-friend followed promptly by her throwing all his stuff out the window, her family occupying his apartment until the airport opened. Jim, Tad, and I laughed at the thought of the Serens caked in grime, squatting in the corner eating beef jerky all by themselves, shouting like ignorant cavemen at anyone who might dare offer them help.

Still, he made himself useful. His main job was boiling water for our guests, either to drink once cooled or bathe with when warm, all made possible by Tad securing a single generator from a friend who left the island shortly before the storm.

Thanks to that generator, we could cook and keep our lights on at night, and taped the switches on all ceiling fans to make sure the guests wouldn't tax the generator too hard. We even charged our cell phones, although there was no signal or internet to reach the outside world.

Calder left before sunrise most mornings, joining the teams to clear felled trees from the long, winding road to Hana, hoping that others were working at the same chore from the opposite direction.

He came back at night, exhausted, to enjoy a semi-warm bath I had ready for him, where we washed up, did our laundry, and enjoyed ourselves before joining everyone for dinner.

Despite the idea that Jeff was still somewhere on the island, things were as perfect as life on Maui could be. Part of me felt this was what native tribes did before the United States invaded and stole their land. The island inhaled compassion and exhaled the aloha spirit everyone expected. Even when the largest hotels opened again, our guests collectively agreed to "stay with Auntie."

I scrawled in a notebook our latest figures. With the airport opening the next day and most of our guests departing, we managed to net

$14,000, half in checks paid to Auntie for the room, and a promise from most of our guests that they would surely return in the future.

That meant only $10,000 to go and two weeks to find it. Somehow. Even my father, who stopped by to "check on his investment," looked concerned, leaving quickly after suffering a verbal beatdown by Tad, who assured him he would never get his grubby hands on Auntie's home.

I even joined in on the yelling, something I never dared to do to anyone before, especially my own father.

Still, things weren't all sunshine and daisies. I kept my promise to Auntie. Called into work the day before, Calder escorted me to the market, where I bagged groceries of mostly dry goods, as the supermarket shelves slowly started to empty, awaiting a much-needed arrival of fresh products from the mainland.

There, I spent hours checking every single face I saw, knowing Jeff was still somewhere on the island. If he found me at the school, he could find me at the supermarket, or at the inn, or anywhere else I went.

At the end of the limited-hours shift, Jim walked me back to the inn. Aside from that, the only place I could be at ease for the last three days was my studio apartment, transformed into a haven thanks to Calder. He helped me keep things cleaned, prepared breakfast for us using my kitchenette in the morning, and decorated with island flowers he brought back from Hana Highway after working to clear it all day.

All those good feelings disappeared with every minute that passed in the cold, too-bright police station.

The lights flickered above me as Officer Lanna met us at her desk. At this early hour, the station was practically empty. I heard one of the officers as we came in talking to his colleague about crime being at an all-time low, and how they would all be better off at home or taking the ferry over to Honolulu, which was, according to them, quite the mess.

Officer Lanna was all business, adopting a more professional posture and appearance than most of her counterparts. She got right to business, first by having me explain in explicit detail what happened in the school the night Jeff showed his face, then had me repeat to verify the police report from Atlanta.

"And you haven't seen him since that night?" she asked.

I shook my head. Meanwhile, my foot spazzed involuntarily, tapping out a dance it called "this fucking sucks." That's when Auntie took over.

"So? Have you found the bastard? Locked him up? Why aren't you doing anything? My nephew can't go anywhere alone because of that man! He's terrified! Can't you do something?"

I grabbed Auntie's shoulder to end her rant. "Let her speak."

Officer Lanna seemed justifiably frustrated. She slid her chair to face me directly. "Adam, we tried to locate him. I even issued a BOLO, but there's no sign of him anywhere. I went through the records at the airlines, the car rentals, and the hotels. There's no indication that Jeff Thatcher landed in Hawaii anytime in the last few weeks."

Auntie shrugged my hand off her shoulder. "Are you calling my nephew a liar?"

"On the contrary. We do know he was seen at the school. He used his real name when he signed in, that much is sure. But he didn't provide a real phone number or hotel. Given the state of things, with half the island still inaccessible, there's just no telling where he's staying and what name he's using. Without at least that information, getting a judge to sign off on a TRO, even in family court, is impossible."

"TRO?" I asked.

"Sorry. Temporary Restraining Order. And because he has no arrest warrant in Georgia, we can't arrest him here and extradite him. Despite his dramatics at the school, he didn't break any local or state laws."

"But what about federal laws? You said he used an alias to get here, which means he's traveling with forged identification. Can't you do anything with that?"

"I've already contacted the FBI office in Kapolei. And right now, they have other concerns. Things on O'ahu aren't great. Law enforcement is stretched pretty thin over there. Without more to go on, my hands are tied."

I sighed and stretched my back. I felt every vertebra pop, as though my muscle tension had compressed my entire spine. "So you're telling me there's nothing I can do?"

"I wish I had better news for you. But I promised you I'd see this to the end. I won't stop looking for Mr. Thatcher. We've also tripled patrols around your residence."

Auntie interrupted. "What about getting security detail?"

"If you mean a bodyguard, that's something we don't have the resources or permission to do. I can give you some information on local companies that provide that service, but you'd have to pay for it."

"Don't bother," I said, thinking about what that might mean. "We can't afford it."

Auntie whacked my shin with her cane. "How about you let me decide what we can and can't afford, Makani."

I rubbed my shin and jokingly asked Officer Lanna to arrest her for assault. She only smiled slightly, preferring to maintain her professional tone.

"What I meant to say is there's no need. The police patrol is fine, and even though I'd prefer not to, being around people at all times isn't so bad."

"What about your father? I know he's on the island and works for a real estate developer. Perhaps you could ask him for help with security."

I balked at the idea. There was no way in hell I'd ever ask for that man's help for anything.

"Have you thought about other options? Since Mr. Thatcher is actively stalking you, perhaps you should return to Atlanta and press charges. I looked it up. Since this constitutes aggravated assault, you have time. My guess is they're just waiting for you to prosecute."

Returning to Georgia was an idea I didn't want to entertain. When I first got to Maui, I ran away from a horrible situation. Returning to Georgia would feel like running away from a really good one. Despite Jeff, I was almost at a place in my life where I felt at peace. I had a close relationship with my family, a job and money of my own, a home I loved, new friends, and the possibility of a relationship that was, by all accounts, very good for me.

I had even started feeling more confident in myself than I had before.

"I can't do that, I'm sorry."

"I'd like to say I understand, Adam, but I don't. You have the chance to put this man away for up to twenty years after what he did to you, and with all the evidence stacked against him, it would be an easy case. You wouldn't even have to take the stand. In the case of domestic violence, most judges allow written statements from the victims. You could not only save yourself, but you could also save future victims of his. And trust me, there are always future victims."

I remembered Debbie and how her husband killed her and then took his own life. I felt guilty. If we had planned our escape even days before, if I hadn't been such a coward, the two of us would be here right now. She would know what to do.

"I'm sorry, I just can't. You're asking me to give up what I've accomplished here. I feel more myself than I have in a long time, and going back to the mainland feels wrong."

Officer Lanna leaned back and turned toward her desk. She passed me a document to sign detailing our conversation and her commitments. "Very well. I'll continue to search for Mr. Thatcher. If we find him, I'll get started on paperwork immediately for the TRO and inform the FBI of his location. Just promise me you'll be careful? In situations where stalkers are involved, they always wait until their victim is alone before acting. And don't forget that you can be alone either by yourself or in the middle of a crowd. Make sure you're with people you trust, who know what you're going through."

"Thank you for your help," I said.

Auntie scoffed a few times. I knew she wouldn't be pleased without Jeff's head on a chopping block. She'd even petition the state to legalize the guillotine again and pull the lever herself.

Officer Lanna shuffled some papers together and said her good-byes, leaving Auntie and me alone. A few minutes later, we sat on a bench outside the police station, Auntie not yet ready to go home.

Thanks to Tad always seeming to find the time, Auntie's car waited for us parked at the curb, prepared to run as poorly as it did before it broke down. I guessed the fix involved twine. Or duct tape. Or twine and duct tape. And a few angry whacks with a hammer to the engine.

We sat in silence, enjoying the beautiful day. With the hurricane petering out hundreds of miles away, the climate had returned to normal.

"Can I tell you something I haven't told anyone else?" I asked Auntie.

"Of course, Makani. You can tell me anything."

"Just promise me you'll believe me. It's about that first night when the hurricane just started, and Jeff chased me outside. I saw something weird."

I paused, thinking about how to best explain it. Auntie turned toward me, her curiosity piqued. "What did you see?"

"Well, not something, per se. I saw someone. Around midnight, after hiding in the dugout for a while, the storm almost seemed to stop. And I don't mean it just died down. It felt as though the rain and wind froze, droplets suspended mid-air. I saw a woman standing on the pitcher's mound."

Auntie's expression turned serious. She looked me square in the eyes, raising her sunglasses. "What did this woman look like?"

I went on to explain in detail the woman in red, her long, dark, curly hair, and her Kahili fan. Even more, I told her about my experience on Big Beach and the Night Marchers. Auntie just sat and listened, hanging on every detail.

"Are you sure it was a Kahili fan, and a pink lily?"

I nodded. "Yes, but I'm sure it was all just a dream. I wasn't exactly in my right mind at the time. You always used to joke about the Night Marchers. Perhaps being back to the island was bad for my imagination."

"Rubbish. You know who you're talking to, don't you? You want to know what I think?" she asked.

She didn't wait for me to respond. "I think you're a true child of Maui, like me. You and I always shared a connection to the island, one your mother and even Tad don't have. And I think Maui recognizes that."

"You talk as though Maui is alive."

"But he is, Makani! He is! Just look around you. Centuries of our people have called this island home. Our people have lived and died on this island. We're born from him, and return to him when we die. I like to think Maui protects us by sending us our ancestors when we need them most."

"But stories of people seeing the Night Marchers are a dime a dozen."

"That they are, Makani, but this island is home to thousands of spirits, good and bad. Who's to say they're real or not real?"

"Science, for one."

"Bah! Fuck science!" Auntie pulled out her flask and took a swig.

"Auntie, we're outside the police station!" I was less shocked at her drinking than I was her unexpected cursing. She rarely swore, but when she did, it packed a punch.

"So they can arrest me. I could do with a few nights of good sleep in a comfy jail cell. Are you going to keep interrupting me?"

I gestured for her to continue, crossing my arms, grinning, and shaking my head.

"I think you saw Princess Popoalaea."

"Who?"

"Don't tell me you don't remember Popoalaea! Waianapanapa?"

"Just keep making up words, and I'm sure I'll remember."

"Bah!" she slapped the back of my head. "The legend of the Waianapanapa Caves, Makani, and the tragic Princess Popoalaea's murder by her cruel husband!"

Like Debbie... Almost like me...

"You remember the black sand beach near Hana?"

"Vaguely," I said. "It's been a while."

"Well, when Calder gets that damn road clear, go over there with him and visit her cave. I'm glad you told me about this. I feel more comfortable now I know the spirits are watching out for you."

"Even if there are spirits," Auntie moved to slap me again for heresy, "what can they do?"

"What can they do, Makani? You know the Night Marchers. Just gazing into their eyes is enough to turn your fate to death! I remember a friend's friend's cousin's boyfriend once saw the Night Marchers and ran off a cliff into a pond to be eaten alive by Moho! They never found his body."

"Now I know you're pulling my chain. Moho?"

"Yeah, Moho. The giant lizard spirit."

I laughed at the idea and wondered if Auntie made it up. But I liked the idea of Jeff also running into the woods in the hurricane, falling into a pond, and becoming giant lizard lunch. The thought did cheer me up.

Auntie beamed at me a bright, comfortable smile. "It's good to see you smile again. You're so handsome when you smile."

She pinched my cheek, but I swatted her hand away, faking embarrassment. It felt good to feel good again. When I woke up that morning, I dreaded going to the police station. Having Auntie there made the entire ordeal palatable.

The feeling didn't last. After helping Auntie into the car and crossing around to get in the driver's side. I looked across the street and spotted her, the woman in red.

I reached out to her, beckoned her to wait, but she stood motionless, her cheeks puffy from crying. A man walked by her, almost through her, and I realized what Auntie had said was true. She was a spirit, perhaps even the princess of Waianapanapa beach, Princess Popoalaea. She opened her mouth to speak, but her words were lost on the wind, sounding muffled, as though she were trying to talk through water. Even if standing next to her, I was sure I couldn't make out her words.

A bus went by. When it passed, she was gone, leaving nothing but a fresh pink lily on the sidewalk. Crossing the street, I picked up the flower and looked for her again, curious about why she appeared now, at this very moment. The hairs on my neck stood up. I felt like I was being watched, but not in a dangerous way. It was as though the island was watching me, the sense of it bombarding me from all directions. Maui was giving me a great, big, warm hug.

I knew why she had appeared. Money. The inn. Calder. Missing my family. My father. Jeff. All these things weighed on me, spinning me out of control. Despite what I told Officer Lanna, I had considered taking what money I had and running away again, forsaking my entire life I had started to piece together, just to get away from it all. Seeing the Princess and feeling so close with the island set my mind straight.

I joined Auntie in the car and sat there motionless, the gentle breeze from the downed windows drying my tears.

Awash with emotions, I didn't start the car. I leaned down and buried my head in Auntie's lap like a little boy. I cried as I twirled the lily stem between my fingers. And I felt a fool for doing so, a grown man breaking down in front of a woman who might as well be my grandmother.

She didn't balk at me. She didn't push me off. She whispered sweet words of comfort and stroked the back of my head, then started singing in a broken, aging voice, a soft, harrowing, relaxing song I remembered from my youth she always sang to me when I needed consoling. She, unlike most people in my life, always understood how to comfort me.

14

AFTERNOON 26

STILL OVERWHELMED BY MY EXPERIENCE AT THE POLICE STATION, I DIDN'T know why I decided to go with Calder to Hana. Before the hurricane, I wasn't sure I was ready for any sort of commitment, even a light-hearted romantic one. But I took Officer Lanna and Auntie's advice to heart. If I were to gain any traction in my life, I needed to escape, to get to where Jeff wouldn't think to look for me, and that was no easy task on an island as small as Maui.

I was looking forward to the short trip, though. Despite nearly four weeks on the island, I hadn't seen much of anything beyond Big Beach and Little Beach. I enjoyed the idea of visiting forests and beaches I hadn't seen since I was a child. I always imagined there was something mystical and fantastical about the sites along the road to Hana, unlike any other place on the island. Most of all, I had to visit the spring where Princess Popoalaea was killed. I was too curious not to.

When Calder asked me to join him I leaped at the opportunity, first checking with Jim to see if I could have a few days off from the market now that things were returning to normal.

With windows rolled down, at around 1 p.m., Calder and I pulled out of the parking lot to join the queue of tourists headed for the reopened airport. In truth, I was glad to be rid of them. When tourists came to visit, they stayed for one week to ten days. Like the clouds perpetually lingering over the eastern cliffs of Pu'u Kukui, these tourists were like a force of nature. But when they remained longer, having endured a category five hurricane, I wanted them gone before we started to care about them. I didn't want to miss tourists after they left.

The traffic jam ended an hour later as we rounded the highway toward Hana, coolers in the back of Calder's truck sliding back and forth every time we coasted around a sharp bend.

I had hoped he would explain in detail every landmark we passed if only to refresh my memory, but he was single-minded at the moment. He had no mind for idle chat.

I could tell he was nervous by the way he drove, cold air blasting from the truck's AC just to cool him down as he sped through Hana Highway's narrow twists and turns. He was anxious, worried about his family, and with cell phone service and landlines still down, he hadn't heard any news from them. All we did know was that the road was now open.

We sat there for an hour, wordless. Occasionally, Calder released the steering wheel and held my hand for a moment, only to return his attention to the wheel at the next sharp bend, where he needed to pull over and wait for an oncoming utility vehicle to clear the bridge.

An hour later, we took a break at a rest stop appropriately named "Halfway to Hana." I imagined it would be packed to the brim with tour buses and rental cars on a good day, with a line wrapped around the concession stand of the tiny building. But it, like so many other properties we passed, was still boarded up from the storm.

Calder didn't say anything as he parked his truck, turned it off, and booked it over to the bathrooms. Pulling out his keyring, he unlocked the padlock on the men's room and disappeared inside. I grew nervous and remembered Officer Lanna's warning not to be alone.

Now, in an empty parking lot, I was alone for the first time since my encounter with Jeff. Silence and solitude tugged at me, as though a spirit were pulling the hairs on my neck.

I got more anxious as a car pulled into the tiny parking area. I could only see the shadow of the driver through the mid-afternoon glare and held my breath as the vehicle slid into the spot next to us. I relaxed when an older woman got out, finicking with her keyring the very same way Calder had.

It seemed all the locals had keys to the bathrooms here, and it made sense. It was the only pit stop locals could use as they drove back and forth from Hana to the center of the island.

Calder came out of the bathroom and spotted the woman. The two met halfway between the truck and the concession stand. As they chatted, I could sense his tension washing away. The Calder I first met in the county council parking lot returned to me.

He embraced the woman before returning to the truck, but he didn't turn it on. Instead, he leaned back and breathed a pleasant sigh of relief, taking my hand in his.

"That's my neighbor," he said to me. "They're all right. Not just my family, but everyone. There's some property damage, but no one was hurt."

I tried to be happy for him, on the outside, at least. And I really was, but I was still coming up from the downer that was nearly a panic attack after being left alone. I didn't want to burden him with my problems, so I leaned over and hugged him, if only to hide my face.

A few moments later, we were back on the road after I assured him I didn't need to use the bathroom, and as the afternoon drew on, the second half of the drive turned out to meet my expectations. With fun music blasting from the speakers, Calder told me stories about each and every stop we passed. The stories grew bolder and more adventurous as we approached Hana. He revealed the haunts of his youth for me in great detail. We both had a good laugh at him and his buddies, including Tad, getting caught skinny dipping by local police at night in a semi-popular swimming hole near Hana.

I found myself regretting not having those stories. I was only a child when I moved to Atlanta. We had no beaches or swimming holes, or bamboo forests to get lost in. Compared to Calder, my childhood felt wasted by hours upon hours of television or video games or comic books. Even making friends in Atlanta was hard to do, especially when I began being bused to a school on the other side of the city.

By the time I was in a position to make friends, I couldn't develop close relationships because they all lived miles away from me in an urban landscape, not safe for a child to traverse.

I wished I had what Calder and Tad had. Perhaps I wouldn't have turned out so screwed up.

After ninety minutes of mostly Calder telling stories, we pulled into Hana to the very same view we had in Lahaina, palm trees toppled over or ripped bare of their fronds. The ones that did remain standing leaned peculiarly to one side or the other, shallow roots loosened from the still muddy ground.

We passed house after house, all showing signs of damage, from roofs wrenched from their walls to trees through windows. It seemed very few homes remained unscathed.

I realized then that I didn't know what Calder's living situation was. Did he live with his family, like me, or did he have his own place somewhere in the tiny town?

I gripped the handhold as Calder pressed his brakes and turned off the road into a single parking spot atop a muddy, downhill driveway, parts of it washed away to reveal bedrock. At the top of the driveway, a toppled fruit stand rested in shambles, a hand-painted pineapple sign sticking out of the pile of split timber.

Calder beeped his horn a few times at a woman waving at him from the bottom of the hill, older than him with long, gray hair tied in a ponytail. I couldn't make out her features from a distance, but the way she held herself and smiled suggested she was Calder's mother.

Calder jumped out of his truck and sped down the hill, slipping a few times in what patches of mud remained, where he embraced his mother, before pointing up toward me.

A minute later, Calder's entire family climbed the driveway to greet me.

"It's good to see you again, lad. How's your auntie doing?" Gordon, Calder's father, asked. I was grateful he skipped the part about seeing me sunburned to all hell wearing nothing but a skimpy, dirty towel. I blushed at the thought of two Wright men seeing my bare ass.

As I answered Gordon's question, Calder introduced his mother, Mary, and his little brother, Danny, and his little sister, Mason, both substantially younger than Calder. I guessed they were in middle school. All three were obviously siblings, with the same gait, smile, nose, and hair color, and the hint of ginger in their vibrant, brown hair.

Unlike Calder, though, who was freshly showered and dressed, they looked a little worse for wear. I could tell by piles of broken trees and outdoor furniture, and some tarps blocking their front window, that they had been hard at work cleaning up from the storm.

That didn't stop any of them from being happy. Danny and Mason returned to a game they were playing, scrambling about the yard picking up fallen debris and dragging it into separate piles, competing as to who could make the largest.

The inside of the house was immaculate. Every room looked like it belonged in Scotland, not Maui. They decorated with luxurious, red furniture and dark brown, patterned floors. They had way too many area rugs. I admired an oversized portrait of a much younger Mary and Gordon, her in a brilliant lace wedding dress and him in a kilt with high socks and a tuxedo top. And so much mahogany wood, like a dozen trees felled just to furnish their home.

Sitting on the living room sofa with Calder, I sensed how relaxed he was, his feet kicked up on an ottoman that doubled as a coffee table, next to a stack of newspapers from the UK, the top one dated a few weeks ago.

As Mary and Gordon joined us, both carrying an assortment of refreshments from lemonade to packaged cookies, I could tell by the way they looked at me that they were curious why I was there, only too polite to ask.

I pretended not to notice when Mary sat next to Calder and jabbed him with her elbow, winking her approval at him in a corny, motherly way, and we sat in awkward silence until Calder saved us all.

"Dad, I haven't checked yet. How did the school hold up? When are students going back?"

Gordon stopped nibbling on a cookie and shrugged. "The school got hit pretty bad, some roof damage in the offices. If we had anywhere to go, we would have evacuated when the eye hit us. The gym's fine, though."

"Do they need any help fixing it?" Calder asked.

"I don't know. You two should drive over tomorrow. They might need some heavy lifting done by two strapping lads."

I chuckled a bit at the idea, never really being one for physical labor unless stacking boxes of cheap comic books counted as "heavy lifting." A few minutes later, lemonade and cookies consumed, I was outside with Calder dragging felled trees and branches, and any other non-plastic or metal refuse to a burn pile in the backyard.

I wasn't resentful of the work. I owed Calder after the way he helped us at the inn, and how he'd helped me in the last few days with my own demons. I felt liberated after four days of playing a prisoner in my own home. I desperately hoped that Jeff wasn't able to track me to this side of the island.

But seeing Calder with his family, with me as the odd man out, made me wonder about his motivations for bringing me here. Did he do so because he needed my help, or because he wanted to spend more time with me, or because he felt compelled to help me escape from Jeff?

As I helped him and his siblings collect debris scattered across the yard, I thought about how I felt about Calder. Sure, he was a nice guy, both strong and gentle, and I was very fond of him, but the whole Jeff fiasco prevented me from feeling anything more.

I was almost grateful when we were done with our work for the day. Calder led me inside to show me to a guest room. He left me there to clean up in a private bathroom to the sounds of a whole-house generator running outside. It suddenly sank in that their home was one of the more grand houses on the island that I'd seen. I didn't know what Mary or Gordon did for work, but I knew the taxes on the land and property would be in line with some of the multi-million dollar homes elsewhere.

I was surprisingly happy that I had my own room, feeling it would be strange to share Calder's bedroom in his parents' house. I still didn't know if Calder actually lived with them, or if he had his own house or an in-law suite in the current home.

To be honest, aside from knowing he teased me as a child, that he was a gym teacher in Hana, and that he was handsome and kind, I didn't know that much about him. We hadn't really talked that much.

After my first hot shower in a week, I lay on the bed in my towel, looking at my phone, hoping the cell signal would be restored soon. I needed to talk to my mother and sister. I wondered what they would make of all of this. In truth, they would probably order me back to Atlanta, something I would never do. I fully intended never to set foot in that city again.

A minute later, I was fully dressed in shorts and a clean t-shirt and downstairs, idling with the family at the base of the driveway as they prepared to leave.

"Where are we going?" I whispered to Calder.

"It's a surprise," he said through a rather cute smile. "You're riding with me."

I was dumbfounded as we skidded up their still muddy driveway and turned right, heading back toward the road to Hana. I grinned after Calder quickly took a right turn off Hana Highway and onto Wai'anapanapa Road, and realized he was taking me to Wai'ana-panapa State Park. We were going to the black sand beach and to the caves where Princess Popoalaea hid from her cruel husband.

It had to have been a coincidence. Calder didn't know about my vision in the dugout or outside the police station. He didn't even know about my hallucination-like experience with the Night Marchers. Going there now felt like Fate had dealt me a good card.

We pulled into the parking lot just as the sun started to set, and stepped out to see a horde of locals flooding the paths leading down to Honokalani Beach, men and women alike carrying coolers, blankets, tents, chairs, and whatever else they needed for an evening cookout.

This was the side of Hawaii that tourists never got to experience. Where they toured the island in air-conditioned buses, sunset cruises, and theatrical luaus hosted by their hotels, they missed out on the local culture of the island that I never experienced in the mainland. Tourists didn't see the community, the family.

It seemed as though the entirety of Hana showed up that night, given the lines of people of all shapes and ages walking down the narrow, uneven path leading to the campgrounds and black sand beach. I trailed behind Calder and his siblings, myself weighed down by a cooler and a camping chair.

Stopping briefly, I looked down the path leading toward Waiana-panapa Cave, and read the sign telling the princess' story:

"Once upon a time, a Hawaiian princess named Popoalaea fled from her cruel husband, the chief Kakae. She hid on a ledge just inside the underwater entrance to this cave. A faithful serving maid sat across from her fanning the princess with a feather kahili symbol of royalty. Noticing the reflection of the kahili in the water, the chief Kakae discovered Popoalaea's hiding place and killed her. At certain times of the year, tiny red shrimp appear in the pool, turning the water red. Some say it is a reminder of the blood of the slain princess."

I wanted to follow the sign, to see and talk to the princess, but the sounds of children splashing in the cave's swimming pool suggested I should return later. Speeding up to a quick jog, I caught up to Calder and Mason, who were already setting up at the top of the hill, both joking around as they tried to lay down blankets stubbornly caught in the wind.

I inhaled the fresh ocean air as I peered down the hill. A winding path worked its way around the hillside, spilling out onto a tiny black sand beach where more groups set up camp around a small bonfire. I could hear the sounds of parents yelling at their children not to go too deep into the water, and they were right to. Every Hawaiian knew if you wanted to avoid becoming shark food, you don't offer yourself as shark bait at sunrise and sunset, optimum feeding time. After dark, swimming needed to be reserved to fresh-water holes and pools, although few native islanders could afford a swimming pool of their own, or justify the expense with the island surrounded by such pristine, blue water.

Most, however, were content just sitting on the beach as the warm waves swept over their feet, admiring the golden glow of the sunset sky. Looking to the east, I spotted the first twinkling stars appear on the horizon, and for a moment, just a moment, I forgot about all of my troubles.

Then Gordon broke the mood as he dropped the wheel of a charcoal grill on my foot. I winced and yanked my foot away, leaving my slipper behind.

"Sorry, lad. Never been great with all this camping stuff."

As I leaned against a boulder and rubbed my big toe, I thought again about what Gordon did for work. What possible job could compel someone to leave Scotland and move to the other side of the world?

"It's okay," I said. "I meant to ask you, Gordon, how did you become friends with my aunt?"

Gordon stroked the gray scruff on his chin. "To be honest, I've forgotten how we met. We've been friends for so long, it just seems like we've known each other forever. Longer than you've been alive, at least."

"So, you know my mother as well?"

"Aye. Your mother used to work as a clerk at the observatory, long before we had cell phones and internet. Her job was to deliver supplies to us and return research materials to ship to the university."

"You worked up on Haleakala?"

"Still do. How's your mother faring, by the way? I'm ashamed for not asking."

I recalled a moment in my childhood, of my mother taking me with her on one of her runs 'up the volcano' to the observatory, and realized she was making a delivery run for him. It was one of the last remaining memories I had on Maui before my father yanked us over to the mainland.

"She's good. I haven't talked to her since before the hurricane, though."

"Really? You want to?" Gordon reached into a deep pocket in his windbreaker and pulled out a massive cell phone with a thick, long antenna — a satellite phone, or so I guessed. I'd never seen one. I caught the glimmer of a "Property of the University of Hawaii" sticker on the back of it as he tossed it to me.

"That's really long distance. Are you sure it's okay?"

"Nonsense! It's a sat phone. The whole planet is in distance. Talk as long as you want to."

Holding the phone to my chest and thanking him, I snuck up the trail for some privacy. I caught Calder smiling at me as he worked on setting up a portable grill while the rest of his family started cooking.

I smirked back as I began punching in my mother's number, hoping she would pick up even though it was close to midnight. I was surprised when, instead of just her digits, the name "Luana Frost" appeared on the screen. Gordon had not only called my mother before but added her to his list of contacts.

In truth, I shouldn't have been surprised. I smiled after realizing that the world was a much smaller place than I had comprehended. Aside from Auntie, I had no clue who on Maui my mother still spoke to.

"Gordon? Is everything okay?" my mother asked, not bothering to say "Hello?" or "Who is this?"

"Mom, it's me."

"Adam! I've been trying to reach you. Is everyone okay?"

I swallowed through a lump in my throat, tasting a bit of metal as I chewed on my lip too hard. "Yes. Everyone is fine…"

"Dear, I know you. Something's wrong. What is it? Why are you calling from Gordon's phone?"

As I hesitated, my mother seemed to know how to handle me. She patiently waited. I could hear her breathing through the phone and sounds of her bedroom fan blowing in the background.

"Mom, he's here. Jeff found me. He's on Maui."

There was another long pause, this one filled with the sounds of clanking and tapping and sliding and clapping.

"Mom, what are you doing?"

"What do you think I'm doing? I'm packing. I'll be on the next flight out."

"That's crazy. You have work and Maria, and you can barely afford to pay rent."

"You don't think I haven't saved enough for an emergency? My baby needs me. Nothing is more important. Anyhow, your sister will be fine. She's a grown woman and can do without her mother for a few weeks."

"What about work? Won't they fire you?"

"If they do, they do. I can always get a new job. Now, no arguments! If I hurry, I can catch the morning flight. I'll see you at the inn tomorrow. And don't go anywhere alone until I get there!"

I felt a single tear slide down my cheek, collecting in the corner of my mouth, triggered by the feeling of a weight lifting off my shoulders. The fact that my mother would drop everything just to be with me brought me so much relief. I knew there was no stopping her. If anything, trying to stop her would make her more adamant. Aside from her spontaneous move to Atlanta decades ago, no one ever told my mother what to do.

"Thanks, Mom. I'm in Hana now with Gordon and Mary. I'll head back home tomorrow morning. I love you."

"I love you too, honey. Just stay safe until I get there. I have to go now. I'll see you soon."

With that, the line went dead. I clutched the phone against my chest again, this time cherishing it like it was a lifeline. So long as I had my family, things would turn out all right.

As I returned to the campsite, I did my best to wipe the tears from my face and clear my nose. I didn't want to sour the mood by having everyone know I had been crying. I was met first by Danny, who eagerly took the phone from me and returned it to his dad.

I then saw Gordon and Mary whispering to one another. Mary shot me a painful, sad look that I was all too familiar with. It was the same look Calder had, and Tad, and Jim, and Auntie, when they first found out about Jeff.

It drove home the idea that Calder didn't just invite me because he wanted to spend more time with me. He was participating in the scheme to keep me safe from Jeff. I wasn't angry at him for telling his parents, either. I felt more disappointed. A small part of me had hoped he invited me with no other ulterior motive.

I felt him creep up beside me and lace his fingers around mine. I slid back, leaning slightly into him, mindful to keep the PDA to a minimum. I wasn't sure how out he was to his family and felt somewhat uncomfortable being completely open with people I had just met.

"I'm sorry. I tell my parents everything. I had to tell them about what you're going through."

"It's fine. I suppose the more people who know, the better."

"You're not mad at me?"

"Not in the slightest. I'm just tired. It's been a long day."

"It's been a long week."

I laughed a little. It really had. But if someone were to ask me while looking out over a hillside of people grilling meat and veggies, and drinking beer and punch, I wouldn't have been able to tell them the island had just been ravaged by a category five hurricane.

Everyone in Hana had work to do to clean up from the storm. But they managed to clean up the park instead, so that the community could have somewhere to go to be, well, a community. Leave it to Hawaiians to turn a bad situation into an excuse for a cookout.

"Can I get you anything?" Calder asked.

"No. I'll have a beer when everyone is ready to eat. For now, I'll just relax. There are enough people here where I finally don't have to worry about Jeff."

Most of the locals had already set up and were starting to cook food. Looking up the trail behind me, the path to Waianapanapa Cave was empty. Conveniently, it was also the closest path for us to get to the bathroom. If I were to have any meaningful encounter with the woman in red, it would be now. I took a step away from Calder and turned to head up the path.

"I need to use the bathroom and get some air. I'll be back."

"You want me to go with you?"

"I think I can manage. Anyhow, it looks like your dad could use you."

I pointed over to Gordon, struggling with the grill. Smoke billowed as he lifted the lid, about ready to put on the meat. He coughed as he inhaled the smoke and dropped the cover. As it clanked on the ground, drawing the attention of Calder's entire family and some of the families around us, I slipped away.

Eager to get to the cave, I hopped up the trail until it forked, one direction leading to the parking lot and the lavatories and the other down the hillside to Princess Popoalaea's spring. When I arrived, I was pleased to find it empty.

The spring reflected the silver moon above, already high in the sky and nearly full. I felt a sense of foreboding as I climbed down deeper.

The entire back of the cave was cast in complete shadow, making it appear more like a bottomless abyss. As I got closer, I cringed a little when I spotted traces of red in the crystal clear water, and wondered if it was really due to baby shrimp or if the legend was true. Was the pool actually saturated with her blood?

There was no sign of the princess. Instead, I was greeted by a chill coming from the ice-cold water below. Where the warm evening air met the frigid water, a layer of steam formed that blanketed the entire cave, only to rise out and be blown away by the trade winds.

I folded my legs and sat on a flat rock, just a foot away from the water's edge, and closed my eyes. I hoped that if I remained long enough and still enough, she would appear to me. If I couldn't talk to her here, I knew I couldn't speak with her anywhere, and I desperately wanted to. I needed to understand why she was helping me. Why she, and the Night Marchers, were appearing to me.

Knowing I didn't have too much time before Calder came looking, I silently prayed for any sign from her.

Five minutes passed. Then ten. Then fifteen. Bordering on impatience, asking with my mind and aloud for the princess to appear, I was about to give up. I had to get back to the others. As I reached in the dark for a handhold to lift my way out of the grotto, I heard a drum beat that sent chills down my spine. I looked for the source, thinking someone down on the beach was playing a war drum. Then another, this one closer. Then another, just up the path. I squinted through the shadows, remembering the very same drums on Big Beach, when I saw the marchers, but didn't spot any torches or ghostly spirits.

I gasped when a red light cast in the grotto behind me, reflecting on the water, causing shimmering patterns to flow over the rocks as though blood were pouring from them. Hesitating, I began to spin to face the light when I felt a powerful force lock my torso, as though an intense rush of water had pinned me to the rocks.

"You mustn't turn around," a woman's voice echoed from behind me, as though she were speaking through a thick veil. "I can speak to you, or you can look upon me. I don't have the power to offer both."

"Who are you?" I asked.

"You know who I am."

"Princess Popoalaea."

"Yes. I was once Popoalaea. Whether I will be again is unclear."

With every word she uttered, the red light pulsed, diminishing only when she was silent. I guessed she was waiting for me to ask my questions. I resisted the urge to turn around. "Why are you appearing to me?"

"Because we are the same. I am now 'Lima Akau O Pele,' the right hand of Pele, tasked with shielding the innocent and enacting revenge on violent lovers, just as Pele enacted revenge on my husband for murdering me. And just as I was Popoalaea, and you are now Popoalaea in this place. I was sent to be your shield, to protect you, child of Maui."

"How do you know what I've been through? It happened so far from here."

"Because Pele reads your thoughts, is poisoned by your fears, and is haunted by your nightmares. The moment your feet touched Maui, you became Pele's ward. So long as you are out of balance, Maui is out of balance. You will never find your home here until Pele is satisfied."

I squeezed my eyes shut, realizing her words were true. Despite my desperate desire to make Maui home once again, to love it as I did as a child, the magic was gone. Jeff stole that from me. I wanted it back.

"What do you need me to do?"

As the blood light pulsed brighter, the wind picked up, causing me to shiver. I felt her cold hand, the chill of it piercing through my shirt like a block of ice was pressed against my shoulder. "Child, even Pele cannot pierce the veil into the future. I need you to be strong, and believe that when you need us most, my marchers and I will be there, to unite our strength with yours."

I chuckled, causing the hand to withdraw from my shoulder, leaving only a burning sensation behind. "My strength? What strength?"

The wind raged around us. I could very much feel Popoalaea behind me, the back of my head, my shoulders, and my back tingling. I slammed my eyes shut and covered my ears, cowering from the sheer power of her. Then it all stopped, and the red light faded to a glimmer.

"Hush! He is here. I can taste his murderous intent on the breeze."

My heart skipped a beat, then surged in my chest. I immediately felt terrified, prepared for a panic attack to come on at any moment. I heard rustling from further up the trail and pleaded to God, Pele, the princess, or whoever might listen to protect me. Calder, Tad, Auntie, Mom, my sister, and even Jim flashed across my mind. I didn't want to leave them now, but I was exhausted. Perhaps it was better to end this, one way or another.

Before I could reach up to climb to the trail to face Jeff or run, I felt something grab hold of me. No. It didn't capture me. It possessed me, controlling me like a puppet. Instead of climbing up, I slid down gracefully into the water, until an invisible current took hold of me and pushed me deeper into the cave.

The princess' voice whispered from behind me. "Remain here. I will hide you. Do not make a sound, or the illusion will break."

The glimmering red light disappeared completely, then a thin wall of water formed around me, rising out from the spring, only for a blast of air to rise from behind me, freezing the water in mid-air.

And like the water, I froze in place, dumbstruck by the princess' power and horrified that Jeff found me.

How did he find me?

I held my breath when I spotted him coming into view, first a pair of heavy hiking boots, then a long, thin pair of jean-clad legs. And at last, illuminated by moonlight, the entirety of him.

He had a sinister, maniacal look on his face, his eyes widened with purpose and malice. He rested his hand on something held securely at his waist. The moon reflected off it, causing it to glisten to reveal its shape, a silver pistol.

"I know you're close, Adam. You wouldn't be too far away from that fat fuck of a lover you found. Why don't you come out and talk to me? I have a present for you that I know you'll love." Jeff spat out every word in the same spiteful, deranged way he did in Atlanta when he beat me to a pulp.

My heart pounded. My lungs burned. The sight of the gun made me dread what might come next, and I stepped back further into the grotto, my slippers catching on a rock, causing me to slip and splash before balancing against the back wall.

The sound wasn't loud enough to break the illusion but drew Jeff's attention as he knelt down and peered into the grotto. He held up a large flashlight, shining it down into the cave.

While the light nearly blinded me, it didn't seem enough to overwhelm Popoalaea's magic. The moment seemed like it would go on forever. All Jeff needed to do was pull out his gun and shoot in the cave to kill me. He had me literally pressed against a wall with no escape. I didn't want to die. But escaping death seemed impossible.

Even submerged in ice-cold water, I felt beads of sweat forming on my brow. The pressure of the moment boiled up from within me, causing my vision to narrow. I felt nauseous and knew if the moment didn't end, if the threat didn't pass, I would faint.

And then luck returned to me. Amidst the dead silence, I heard the pitter-patter of tiny feet and the laughter of children coming up the trail from the beach and spotted four flashlights flickering about to light their way.

The presence of others was enough to chase him away. As he bounded up the trail, his thick boots pounding against the stone above my head, I could breathe again. The illusion still held as my four saviors zoomed by, two children and two adults, all oblivious of what just occurred.

Once their voices faded completely, the water unfroze and splashed down around me. Warm air rushed into the tiny cave.

Then, in her full majesty, Popoalaea appeared before me. She floated above the spring, her majestic red dress cascading down to barely graze the water's surface. I knew she couldn't talk to me, but the way she smiled, just as she had outside the school during the hurricane, told me I was safe. For now.

15

MORNING 27

I AWOKE FROM A FITFUL SLEEP AS THE GENERATOR OUTSIDE THE GUEST room roared to life. Recalling what transpired the night before, I vaguely remembered shuffling back to Calder and his family a complete wreck, babbling out what had happened with Jeff, sparing them the details of Popoalaea.

Leaning up, the thin sheet covering me slid down to reveal a red handprint on my shoulder that I hoped Calder didn't see as he undressed me and put me to bed.

I couldn't recall how we packed up. A fierce rumble in my stomach suggested the cookout was a waste. I only hoped I wasn't too nutty in front of Calder's siblings. I wished I didn't scare them, or anyone else for that matter.

Rubbing my eyes, I adjusted to the morning light breaking through the window blinds. On the couch opposite the bed, Calder was still fast asleep. I felt glad he was there, in a 'knight in shining armor' sort of way, but also guilty at the same time. He didn't ask for any of this. Now his entire family was mixed up in all my craziness. They had other things to worry about.

Climbing out of bed, I realized I was completely naked. It made sense. I was soaked to the bone. Pulling my bag off the floor, I picked out the only other change of clothes I had, the ratty pair of jeans I wore when I arrived on Maui, and my favorite t-shirt, a faded red, softer-than-soft shirt with the Flash's lightning bolt on the front.

Sometime between going to the bathroom and brushing my teeth, Calder woke up in a daze, the hair on the right side of his head sticking up vertically in the worst case of bed head I had seen in a long time.

He didn't say anything to me when I walked back into the bedroom. He just stood up, wearing only his sleep shorts, crossed the room, and wrapped me into a warm, tight bear hug.

"Thanks for staying with me last night," I said as I pushed my cheek into his shoulder. I tried to inhale through my nose, to smell that natural scent of his I liked too much, but I was completely clogged up, something that I remembered always happened when I ventured over to the more humid, windward side of the island.

"You gave us quite a scare. I don't know what I'd do if anything happened to you..."

He grabbed me tighter, one arm wrapped around my waist, the other over my shoulder. I didn't want to let him go. "I know. I'm sorry."

"You have nothing to be sorry for. It's not your fault."

He let me go after a knock on the door and moved around to dress as his father peeked into the room.

"Adam. Good, you're awake."

Awake wasn't the word for how I felt. My shoulder still burned hot from where Popoalaea touched me, as though ice were pressed into my skin for an hour, and my temples ached from what I assumed was a mixture of exhaustion and stress.

"I'm sorry about last night, Mr. Wright."

"Gordon, please. And there's no need to apologize. When we got home, we called the police. It seems you have a friend willing to drive all the way to Hana in the middle of the night. Officer Lanna is waiting for you in the den when you're ready."

I thanked him, and he left Calder and me alone. Calder tried to comfort me again, but the tension of the moment compelled me to gently push him away. I didn't need hugs right now. With Jeff still on the run, I didn't deserve them nearly as much as he offered.

"I'm sorry," I said as I began collecting my bag to leave the room. "You were kind to invite me here, but I only managed to put you and your family at risk."

He tried to interrupt me, but I held up a firm finger, surprised at how dominant I was being. I usually let others control a conversation. "Before you say anything, I know you were thinking about it. So did your mom and dad. They're good parents. I wouldn't be angry if they wanted me gone until this is all settled, one way or the other.

"Anyhow, my mother is landing in a few hours. I need to get back to the inn. Let me and my family handle Jeff. Until then, I think you should stay away from me. I don't want you to get hurt."

Calder tapped his foot impatiently, waiting for me to finish, then launched into a rant of his own as he tore about the room dressing himself.

"Good. You're done feeling sorry for yourself and blaming yourself for everything? First, you didn't put my family at risk. Your crazy ex did. And I'm not the kind of guy who leaves a friend hanging out to dry when he's in trouble, especially not a guy I care about as much as you.

"And before you go and suggest that you and your family handle this alone, you should know you've been away from this island for a long, long time. Your aunt and Tad are about as close to family as we have on Maui, and I would rather burn in hell than see anything or anyone hurt them. Now that little family of ours includes you.

"So, sure. You have to see this through to the end. You just don't have to play the damn martyr and go it alone. Until this whole ex thing is taken care of, wherever you go, I go. This is not up for debate. I will not just 'stay away from you.'"

"But what about your family? Your job?" I asked.

"My family will be just fine. As for work, it sounds like the school will be closed for a while. Now, if you're done moping around, we should go talk to Officer Lanna. Sounds like she's been waiting for a while."

I followed Calder out of the bedroom, my overnight bag slung over my shoulder. He led me through to another part of the house I didn't see the day before, a sunken den in the back with a glorious ocean view, a straight line of sight to the rocky coast about fifteen feet below the house's elevation.

I peered in the kitchen as we passed and saw Mary, Mason, and Danny sitting down for breakfast. The kids didn't look fazed at all by what had happened. Danny shot me a giant grin and waved excitedly before returning his attention to his plate.

Down a small flight of stairs to the den, Officer Lanna and Gordon sat, both enjoying steaming cups of coffee, the scent of the bold brew lingering in the air.

Just inhaling the smell was enough to wake me up. As I joined them and sipped on a cup poured for me, Officer Lanna went into detail about everything she had learned since the day before.

"I know it's hard to hear, but we still don't know where Jeff Thatcher is. I flagged his name for dispatch and received a report only twenty minutes after Gordon called the police last night. I was able to set up a roadblock on 360 to check every car coming from Hana, but he didn't take that road. So he's either still in the area, or he managed to drive route 37 around the south side of the island. There's also been no sign of him at Keokea."

"So, we're back to where we started?" I asked.

"Not quite. Thanks to Gordon, I was able to talk to a few people who were at Waianapanapa last night, and they confirmed your report. They did see a man matching Jeff's description open carrying a firearm. One witness saw him leave the parking lot, heading south on Hana Highway toward town and confirmed he was driving a Honda motorcycle. I checked the vehicle theft records and confirmed a motorcycle matching the description was reported stolen from Kahului, very close to the airport. Right now, we're canvassing neighborhood watch leaders across the island and issuing his photograph to all markets and hotels. We've also submitted our report to television and news radio contacts to warn the public. If he's listening to the radio at all, he'll know we're actively searching for him."

"You honestly think that's going to work?" Gordon interjected.

"Throwing a big net over the whole island? Who's to say he's not sleeping rough somewhere? Won't that make him more dangerous?"

Officer Lanna sighed and finished the last of her coffee. I could tell she hadn't slept. She looked worn, with puffy bags forming under her eyes. "That's just as likely, especially since he's not driving around in a car. Either he's slipping by our roadblocks by taking dirt trails, or he's hiding out somewhere in the vicinity. Either way, the fact that he was spotted with a weapon changes things. Do you know if he was legally registered to carry in Georgia?"

I shrugged. Considering only a month ago he tried to murder me, I knew I wasn't the best judge of character when it came to Jeff Thatcher. Until he actually landed me in the hospital, I thought he was just abusive, not homicidal.

"I'll check on his gun permit to determine if it's his weapon or a stolen one. In the meantime, having a weapon is enough justification for me to assign you a police detail. Unfortunately, that means you'll need to return to Lahaina. And don't forget my offer. I can arrange for you to talk to a social worker if you need to. She's no therapist, but she's on our payroll and can help you cope with everything."

Calder reached over and gently squeezed my hand. He did his best to put on a smile and cheer me up some. I rubbed the back of his hand with my thumb as I mulled over Officer Lanna's offer.

"If anything," I said, "I think I have too many people to console with, and my mom will be landing in a few hours and will definitely want to talk my ear off. Thanks, though."

"Fine, but promise me you'll get back to Lahaina quickly. I'd escort you, but my partner wants to canvass Hana for a while to see if we can't track Mr. Thatcher down."

"We'll leave in the next thirty minutes," Calder said.

"Good. I'm glad you're going with him. Once you reach mile marker zero, one of the officers there can escort you the rest of the way back to the inn. Before I leave, do you have any other questions?"

I shook my head as I stared down at my now empty mug, the remains of spent grounds clumped at the bottom. I pretended for a moment it was tea, and I could read the shapes to predict the future. I hoped to see, I don't know, the image of a fluffy bunny to comfort me.

Instead, the only shape I saw was a clump of brown muck. I remembered Princess Popoalaea, and the last words she spoke to me:

I need you to be strong and believe that when you need us most, my marchers and I will be there, to unite our strength with yours.

Now wasn't a time to sulk around feeling sorry for myself. My mother was coming. I had Auntie and Tad and Calder and so many others looking out for me. Jeff had no one. Even the spirits of the island plotted against him. If last night was the bottom of the curve of my life, I had every reason to believe things from here on would lead me uphill.

I stood up and held out my hand, thanking Officer Lanna, and followed Calder into the kitchen to grab some food before we hit the road.

Within thirty minutes, we were back in his truck and pulled out onto Hana Highway. Just as we did, my phone started buzzing like crazy in my pocket as it picked up the first signal since the hurricane.

While Calder drove, I read through message after message and listened to voicemail after voicemail from my mother and my sister. There were also a dozen missed texts from my boss at the Comic Book shop, followed by a last "If you're not dead, you're fired. Don't bother coming in," message.

Then the photos started coming in. First, a picture of me at the supermarket pushing carts, taken from behind a bush. Then a picture of me at the graveyard talking to my mother. Then another picture of Auntie's car engine with Jeff holding a pair of pliers in view. Then a picture of Calder and me talking outside the town hall. The worst photo came last, one of me alone in my room, standing at the window shirtless, taken from the beach only forty feet away.

Jeff sent photo after photo of Calder, Auntie, Tad, and me at every place I had gone, every move I had made since my second week on the island, Jeff always managing to get into my shadow without me even realizing it.

I wondered how he managed to keep track of me. How was he always there? I looked in the rearview mirror and saw no sign of him. I checked through the settings on my phone to make sure I wasn't sharing my location.

Calder weaved his truck left and right along the winding highway as I dropped my phone in the cup holder and began tearing through my bag, the only thing I seemed to have with me most of the time. I pulled out and checked each item I carried, then began searching each pocket of the backpack.

"Adam, what's wrong?"

"It's Jeff! I know he's tracking me somehow. He has to be! There's no way he followed me everywhere."

And then I found it. A line of stitches on an inside pocket. Behind the stitches, I felt a box the size of a flip lighter. I tore at the stitches in vain. "Do you have a pocket knife?"

"Glove compartment," Calder said, eyeing me briefly, concerned.

I tore through the compartment until I found the knife, unfolded it and got to work, slicing one stitch after another until I freed the device, a sleek, black box that flashed green at the side, barely large enough to fit in the palm of my hand and as thin as a credit card.

"I knew it!" I said as I tossed the device out the window. "I don't know when, or how, but he managed to hide a tracker in my bag weeks ago!"

I continued searching the bag for any other hidden devices and breathed a sigh of relief when I came up empty. I tried to feel relieved, but couldn't relax. It was a new bag. When did he have the chance to hide the device? Did he sneak into the inn? Did he get to it while I was at work? Was there one in my old bag as well? There most likely was. Otherwise, how did he find me at all?

A few minutes later, my phone buzzed again, this time with a picture taken from a distance of police cars and officers facing away from him, then another, a selfie of him flashing a gun around the corner from the inn.

"Fuck!" I yelled, causing Calder to swerve the car.

"What's wrong? What is it?"

"He got past the roadblocks!"

With no one behind us, Calder slammed the brakes and pulled to the side of the road. We were only a few miles out from the police checkpoint.

I leaned forward and pressed my head into the dashboard. Jeff was everywhere, threatening everyone I loved. I felt caged, as though he had trapped me in a prison the size of Maui and was prodding me with a stun baton over and over and over again.

Calder rubbed my back to try to calm me down. "What do you want to do?"

"I want to go somewhere he can't find us, somewhere I can think." I jumped as a car zoomed, blaring its horn at the sight of us pulled over on the narrow road. Breathing in and out, I tried to piece together some sort of plan but came up empty.

Calder put the truck back into drive and pulled onto the road again. "I think I know where we can go, but we should stop somewhere safe first to check the truck and make sure he didn't leave any more surprises. And you should call Officer Lanna. If he's in Lahaina, they're wasting time operating the roadblock."

"But how did he even have time to get by them?"

"I don't know. If he's on a bike, I can tell you Hana Highway is pretty easy going. If he left right after you spotted him last night, he could have made mile marker zero before the police got there."

"Okay. Where do you have in mind?"

"The Haleakala Visitor Center. It has food, water, and a place to sleep. It should be empty now, and I have the door code for when I worked there. We can stay there the night and come up with a plan tomorrow morning."

"I don't know. Isn't that kind of risky? If he manages to find us up there, we have nowhere to go."

Calder pulled off the road again, this time at a viewpoint with some parking room at the side and hopped out. "It's up to you, Adam. I can't make the call for you. You need to decide."

As I joined him outside the truck, searching high and low for any sign of a tracking device, I thought about our options. Sure, I could go to the police station. That would make the most sense, but that would just make Jeff go into hiding again. Or worse, he would start targeting my family. So far, the Maui police were great, but the thing about the island was there were plenty of off-the-beaten-path places to hide out, especially with an island low on tourists.

I could trust the police to protect me at the inn. Me being there would turn my whole family into prisoners in their own home.

A rational person would certainly select one of those options. And if anything, Jeff knew that I was always rational. Perhaps it was time for me to take a risk.

After we finished checking the truck, we got back in. "So? What do you want to do?"

"I know it's not the best thing, and it makes no sense, but I need an escape, even for just a night. Let's go to the Visitor Center."

A few minutes later, we reached the police roadblock, where we explained our destination to one informed, but confused cop. Considering the officer had no authority over us, he waved us on. We turned left off the highway and wound our way up route 365 toward the volcano.

Less than a minute later, I received an angry call from Officer Lanna.

"I'm sorry, but for the first time in weeks, he doesn't know where I am! I know Jeff. Once he figures it out, he'll be furious. If you're that worried about us, you can set up another one of your roadblocks on Haleakala Highway or send your police detail up to meet us, but I'm not going back to the inn. I can't put my family at risk."

"Please reconsider, Adam. If you just get to the police station, you can spend the night there. Hell, you can stay over at my house if that'll make you feel safer."

I could tell she was worried, but I was already committed to the irrational decision I made. I really, desperately needed to get away.

"You're kind to offer, really. For now, I just need you to find Jeff. You should be able to do that more easily with me out of the way. Promise me you'll still keep someone at the inn to watch out for my family?"

"Of course, but I'm going to send one of my officers up there next shift to check on you. I can get someone there this afternoon."

"Thank you, Officer Lanna. I'll see you again tomorrow at the station."

"Please stay safe."

"I will. Thanks for all your help."

I hung up just as we turned the bend onto Haleakala Highway, only forty minutes out from the visitor center, taking into account how Calder mastered each and every bend in the road. The way he braked and accelerated around the turns made me feel as though I was in a cross-country road race, sharing a cockpit with Speed Racer.

For the first time in a while, Calder seemed to really be enjoying himself. I hadn't seen him this carefree since the hurricane. I remembered our first chance meeting at the town hall, and how I clung to him as he sped down Honoapiilani Highway on his motorcycle.

Now, only a few weeks later, he was going so far out of his way to protect me. I knew without him, I wouldn't have been able to handle everything going on in my life. That left me feeling both happy and sad, but as we raced up the volcano and put Jeff further and further behind us, I just became content, glad to spend the time alone with him.

16

AFTERNOON 27

W<small>E PULLED INTO THE COMPLETELY EMPTY PARKING LOT JUST BEFORE NOON.</small> At ten-thousand feet above sea level, I struggled to draw a full breath of air. Once the truck turned off, everything went quiet.

I paused for a moment, my bag flung over my shoulder, and admired the eerie nature that was Haleakala in the late morning, and appreciated the idea of strolling through the dense cloud layer clinging to the volcano's peak. I remembered sunrise trips to the summit as a child, lingering with my mother, father, and little sister for hours after the last tour bus left until the martian-like landscape glowing bright red in the morning sun was replaced by thick, dense clouds.

Calder took my hand and led me to the dark, locked up visitor center. The tiny building stood stalwart atop the crater rim, the outer wall fused into a stone barricade where people could safely lean over and look straight into the crater below. Steep cliffs gave way to rocky slopes that extended to the horizon. I looked forward to the view in the morning; that was, if we woke up in time to climb the remaining one hundred feet up to the outlook.

He punched in the door code and led me inside the building, through the tiny foyer offering snacks, drinks, and information brochures, and into the much larger back room, adorned with a table, a full-size couch bed, a kitchenette, and a private bathroom.

My imagination ran away with me as I pictured us living here forever, waking up every morning to the most majestic view on the planet, and filling our days with simple things for a simple life — romance and sweets and POG. If only life were that easy. If only I didn't need money to get by.

As I looked out the picture window into the cloudy landscape, Calder eased himself behind me and wrapped his arms around my waist. I shuddered as he kissed my neck, his lips bringing warmth to the cold, gray room.

Just to wrap things up, to completely disconnect from the world, I unlocked my phone and shot a text message off to my mother, telling her where I was and apologizing for not meeting her until tomorrow, then tossed it onto the table next to us.

I faced Calder, standing on the balls of my feet and wrapping my arms around his neck to pull him down into a sweet, sensual kiss. Being this close to him sent chills down my spine, and reminded me of our first kiss in the greenhouse with the storm swirling around us.

As he peeled my hoodie off, goosebumps formed on my forearms. He took each arm in turn and kissed upward from my wrist to my neck, then reached down and slowly peeled off my shirt.

With him still dressed and me half-naked, I felt exposed, but I didn't care. I reached down and yanked his shirt over his head in one awkward, sad motion like I possessed the grace of a manic puppy. Calder laughed as he untangled himself and picked me up with a brute force that was both firm and gentle.

He carried me to the couch, my thighs hitched over his forearms and sat down, so I was straddling him. I dove in, and we made out with ferocity and desire. The rest of our clothing seemed to discard themselves, scattered throughout the room with complete disregard.

Calder continued to kiss my neck as I inhaled his pleasant scent, the same smell of earth and sweat and sunscreen like he had spent time gardening on a chilly, cloudless morning. Petrichor—the smell of dust after rain.

I admired how he paid attention to every inch of my body. Rolling over, so I sat on the couch, he slid down to his knees and took me into his mouth. My back stiffened. My thighs ached from spasm after spasm, his hot breath, and the cold air in the room alternating. Mixing in the thin air at this elevation, I started to feel lightheaded. Just as my body yearned for more oxygen, it also craved more of him.

Lubricated enough by his saliva, he switched positions until he lay on top of me, bracing his weight with one arm while grabbing both our cocks in his large hand while his hips gyrated and bucked back and forth.

The variety of his rhythm, his change of grip, and the rubbing and grinding pushed me to the edge. I knew we were both getting close.

I wrapped my arms around him and locked his lips to mine as he continued to rock back and forth. Moan after moan escaped me until I crossed the threshold and lost control. We both trembled simultaneously as we erupted, covering me from my pelvis to my neck. Our concurrent orgasms lasted well over thirty seconds, a silly, explosive frenzy of springing and trembling and moaning and panting until Calder collapsed into me, both of us gasping for air.

And, like most men do after sex, we let out our single "that was good" laugh, pleased with ourselves for doing such an excellent job.

Calder didn't bother to clean me up right away. He slid sideways onto the couch and spooned me, continuing to kiss my neck and shoulder. Then, when our euphoria passed, he grabbed a roll of paper towels and cleaned us up before settling back down, covering us with a bedspread he claimed from a nearby wardrobe.

As we lay there, we didn't say anything. I was glad for that. I didn't want to talk about the past or the future. I just savored the present, eager to take complete advantage of our little escape from the chaos ten-thousand feet below.

I didn't know when I fell asleep, but when I woke up, Calder wasn't next to me. Lights were on, and the room was considerably warmer. A generator buzzed and vibrated from outside that powered the lights. The heat came from a wood stove in the corner of the room that doubled as a cooktop. Steam rose from a pot on the stove with two discarded ramen containers sitting empty on the counter.

The table was cleared and set. My clothes were neatly folded, piled on the coffee table with my phone on top. A clock on the wall read 3 p.m. I had napped for a little over two hours.

I wondered how Calder managed to set everything up without waking me. More so, my stomach wondered when I was going to eat again. I hadn't had anything since breakfast, and the smell of boiling noodles and spices egged me on.

Calder came in from the lobby just in time to stir the noodles before they boiled over. With the finesse of a novice chef, he tried to stir the water, spilling some out the side, cursing as some boiling water splashed onto him.

I laughed, not because he screwed up but because, for the first time since I met him, I caught him doing something he didn't really know how to do. But he tried, and that was enough for me. Jeff never tried. Even if I worked at the store until six at night, he expected me to have food ready and waiting for when he got home from happy hour. If there was one take away from my destructive relationship, it was learning how to work a kitchen.

I put on my clothes, crossed the room, and urged Calder out of the way. "You've done enough. Let me."

Looking down at the sad state of the packaged ramen, I was glad only for the fact that they were the authentic variety, not the tiny styro-foam cups most college kids nuked in their microwaves.

Opening the cupboard, I found an unopened stick of pepperoni, a jar of pickled artichoke hearts, and a can of pickled heart of palms. It didn't take much to rinse the vinegar off the vegetables and add them to the pot, add some chunks of pepperoni, and mix in the spices, the outcome was certainly better than a cup of boiled noodles with spice powder.

"Thanks," Calder said as I set two bowls down on the table.

"Looks like I'll be doing the cooking from now on?"

"I don't know. I can work a grill just fine."

I smiled at him as we both slurped down our noodles. I recalled some short relationships I had before Jeff, and how they shared in common what I experienced with Calder now. That quiet awkwardness of two people who know one another well enough to be intimate, but not well enough to be at ease. I didn't want to sour the mood by saying the wrong thing, making the wrong joke, or putting myself out there first, and I suspected Calder felt the same. His eyes looked at everything in the room but me.

We weren't like this after the hurricane when we shared my apartment. We were too exhausted around bedtime to do anything but shower, fool around, and pass out. Now truly alone for the first time, I didn't know how to be together with just him. Calder's patience and kindness didn't make it any easier.

"What are you thinking?" Calder asked me.

I finished the last slurp of my noodles, looked up at him, and cleared my throat. "Actually, I was just thinking about how lucky I was to meet someone as kind as you."

"That's sweet. Cheesy, but sw—"

A loud bang followed by the lights flickering interrupted him. A few more booms caused the generator to shut down. The lights went off for good. The room felt cold and unwelcoming again, like all life and love and goodness were sucked out of it. No more our private sanctuary, the tiny staff room at the top of the volcano, to me, immediately felt like a trap.

"Adam Frost! Come out! I know you're in there!"

While I froze in place, recognizing Jeff's voice immediately, Calder sprung into action.

"Enough of this!" he said as he stormed out. I chased after him, pleading with him to just lock the doors, but something took hold of him. I'd never seen him angry before, and I didn't like it. Anger and rage were Jeff's domain. Calder was too gentle, too kind.

I followed him outside and caught my first sight of Jeff in broad daylight. I knew immediately he had snapped. His normally kempt hair and shaven face had grown out. He looked like the total lunatic and sociopath that he proved himself to be, and his arms, face, and clothes were caked in dirt.

"What the fuck is wrong with you? Why can't you just leave him alone!" Calder walked toward Jeff, who stood next to Calder's truck, the tires slashed so we couldn't escape. In barely enough time for me to blink, Jeff didn't say a single word. He just raised a gun and discharged a single shot. Next thing I knew, Calder staggered on his feet before he collapsed into a heap, face-first on the ground.

I let out a guttural scream, laced with rage and fear and malice. It shook me, lasting until my voice cracked. Jeff just smiled, moving Calder's head around with his foot.

"Leave him alone!"

"Please, like I care about this fat fuck." He kicked Calder in the gut before moving past him, directly toward me. "None of this would have happened if you just came with me that night at the school. But no! You just had to go to the police. You just had to ruin everything!"

"Ruin everything? You put me in the hospital! You ruined my life in Atlanta, and now you're ruining my life here!"

I stepped backward until I was pressed into the stone barrier overlooking the crater. I thought about running inside but didn't know the punch code.

Jeff let out a demented chuckle, his eyes blazing and full. He looked like an anime villain. "What life? You had no life! What? Your dead-end job as a shop boy? Dinner with your whore of a mother and that bitch you call a sister? Without me, you'd most likely be sleeping in the streets! You're worthless. Your whole family is worthless. All of you should be put out of your misery! You're nothing but a waste of space!"

He raised his gun and fired toward me, but missed. My heart stopped. I'd never had a gun fired at me before. Hell, aside from the police, I'd never even seen a gun in person before. I moved in the only direction I could, toward the trail leading up to the overlook.

"Go ahead. Run. I'll give you a head start," Jeff said as he reached into his pocket and pulled out some bullets. He flipped the part of the revolver open that held them. I didn't know what it was called. I didn't know anything about guns whatsoever. I just knew he was out of ammo, and that meant I had time.

"No! I'm done running!"

I charged at him, thinking about nothing more than ending this so I could get help. I needed to save Calder. Reaching for the gun, I grabbed it and yanked it down with all my might, but Jeff was too strong. Although bullets flew everywhere, he was able to yank the gun away from me and drove the grip down directly onto my shoulder, then pushed me to the ground.

I winced as pain overwhelmed me, then keeled over as Jeff delivered a swift kick to my gut. While he stepped away to pick up the bullets and finish loading the gun, I rose to my feet, only for him to fire a single shot that struck me in the thigh.

I didn't know whether it was the shock of his assault or the adrenaline rushing through my body, but I didn't feel much more than intense pressure. I looked down and saw blood flowing down my pant leg. I closed my eyes, knowing this was the end, but that moment never came. It took every ounce of willpower I had to partially open one eye to find that time had practically stopped. Bullets that were rolling around the ground stood in place. Wisps of smoke from Jeff's gun lingered in the air, and Jeff's mouth was wide open as he was stuck shouting out his rage.

Then I felt her presence behind me. The woman in red. Princess Popoalaea. And I heard drum beat after drum beat, in perfect rhythm with my own pounding heart.

"We can linger for only a minute," she whispered in my ear. "It's up to you to finish this."

"But I'm not strong enough," I said, looking at the raging maniac that was my ex-boyfriend, suspended in time.

"Yes, you are. I wouldn't be here if you weren't. I'm only able to help people who already have the power to save themselves. I'm here to give you the courage I lacked so long ago. You must fight!"

The flow of time resumed in a way that left me dizzy, and an explosion of red and blue lights appeared behind me, mixing together in a cascade interrupted only by my long, drawn, shadow. In an instant, I felt all my pain disappear. A power grew in me, becoming stronger and stronger as drums beat faster, with more fervor and ferocity, in tune with a Night Marcher's war chant.

I couldn't help but smirk when I realized Jeff could see it all. And he freaked out.

"What the fuck!?"

As I stepped forward, with Princess Popoalaea and the Night Marchers at my back, he raised his gun. I should have lost my nerve, but I didn't. I felt confidence surge through me as I marched among the ranks of the greatest warriors Hawaii had ever known. I was a child of Maui. And I would be damned if an asshole like Jeff Thatcher took that away from me.

He fired round after round at the nightmarish apparitions. I continued moving forward as I heard them zip by me. Even after he had drained the gun of every bullet, he continued to pull the trigger as if more would magically appear, then he hurled the gun toward them. This only intensified the chant, the words and meaning of it lost to me. I immediately regretted so much that I had lost. Thanks to my father, I was torn away from my homeland, my people, my culture. Thanks to Jeff, I lost all my self-worth. I had completely forgotten what it was to be a part of a proud people with traditions so ancient they were more legend than fact. But with my ancestors at my back, I knew I had power and courage and fortitude enough to fight back. Hundreds of generations of it sprung from the ground, through me, and around me. Jeff could never take that away.

The marchers picked up the pace to match my sprinting, straight at Jeff. The ground seemed to shake with every footfall. As I got close, I adopted the pose of the warriors at my side. I lowered my shoulder and flung myself into him with all the force I could muster, sending him flying.

The Night Marchers rushed by me and enveloped him in a frenzy, like sharks going crazy at the scent of blood in the water. Through the haze of their bodies, I saw him screaming and thrashing, gasping for air as he continued to stagger toward the edge.

I raised a single hand toward him, not sure what to do, as I watched him tumble over the waist-high wall and plummet into the crater below. Then, as though I were in a clandestine dream, the Night Marchers vanished. Princess Popoalaea was gone. Jeff was gone, leaving nothing but an empty gun, a scattering of fallen bullets, and a single pink lily on the ground.

With them gone, their power seemed to drain from me. I could feel the bullet hole in my leg. It burned like a bitch, as though lava had run over my thigh. I staggered over to Calder and struggled to the ground, turning him over until he was lying in my lap.

"Please, no. You can't die," I cried. Tears fell from my eyes all on their own. I didn't will them to fall. They offered themselves up at the sight of Calder's lifeless body.

I didn't know what to do. Our phones were locked inside. I searched in vain for Jeff's car, only to find a motorcycle hidden behind some boulders at the front of the parking lot. Knowing I couldn't use it to transport Calder, even if I had the keys, I prayed to anyone able to help.

God. Pele. Popoalaea. Maui! I still need you!

With the sleeve of my hoodie, I put pressure on his wound while I leaned my head back, breathing through the pain radiating from the hole in my leg, a painful ribcage, and a sore clavicle, hardly the worst injuries inflicted on me by Jeff Thatcher. But now, finally, to be the last. I cried. My emotions of panic and relief fused together into a profound release. It was over, and if I could get some fucking help, I could start to live my life again.

17

AFTERNOON 31

MORGUES WERE A STRANGE PLACE TO BE. I'D NEVER BEEN IN ONE BEFORE. I didn't know what to expect going in. But with Officer Lanna on one side, Tad on the other, and Auntie and my mother waiting out in the hallway, I knew I wasn't alone in facing down this tough moment.

I couldn't bring myself to step within five feet of the covered body in front of me, nor was anyone expecting me to. I could feel their concerned eyes on me. They steadied me more than the crutches painfully digging into my armpits, and they offered their support the entire way down to the morgue from my hospital room.

"You don't need to do this," Officer Lanna had said only minutes before after I asked her to see his body. "Everyone will understand if you just want to put this behind you."

And now I knew she was right. I didn't need to do this. The chill of the dark morgue chased away most of my resolve. But I needed closure. I needed to know for sure that it was true, that the nightmare of the last few years of my life was over. I only wished it hadn't cost me so much.

Tad caught me as my grip slipped on one of my crutches. I looked back at him and saw a slight smile, a reassuring "you got this, bud," sort of look that egged me on.

"Go ahead. I'm ready," I said to the coroner, a slight man in his sixties who proved more than amiable to my request to see the body.

With little hesitation, he pulled the white linen sheet down that covered the remains, only to the neck, and I saw what I had wanted to see since the moment I heard the news.

When Officer Lanna joined my family in the hospital room to let me know the search and rescue helicopter had returned with his body, part of me remained steadfast in denial. They couldn't be right. I wasn't that lucky.

But then again, I was. I breathed a sigh of relief at the sight of Jeff's face, hidden behind scrapes, bruises, and contusions inflicted on him as he tumbled down the steep slope into the basin that made up Haleakala's crater. With his swelling and bruising and deformity, and his puffy, blue, lifeless skin, his demise was an absolute certainty. I won. Jeff Thatcher was dead. I was officially a domestic violence survivor. Unlike my dear Debbie, I was not a faceless statistic. Now I could start to breathe again. I could begin to live my life.

"Thank you, Officer Lanna. Is there anything else you need from me before I go?"

"Not at all. Is there anything you need from me?"

"Just… Tell Calder's family I'm sorry, that I wish none of this ever happened."

She agreed, said her goodbyes, and escorted us out of the room. As I left the dank morgue for the brighter hospital hallway, greeted by Auntie and my mother, I immediately felt restored. My whole family except Maria was with me. And even she was on her way to the island. Tad and I promised each other we would hound her incessantly until she agreed to stay.

As we got into the car, Auntie and Tad in the front and my mother and me in the back, I felt a desperate need to talk about anything else. The Estate Inn came to mind and our outstanding obligation. Ten thousand dollars to pay the tax bill. And who knew how many thousands of dollars in medical expenses I managed to rake in.

"I just can't wait 'til Maria gets here!" Mom chimed in as Tad pulled out from Maui Memorial Medical Center.

"What's the point?" Tad interjected. "We still only a week away to you and Auntie being homeless. Unless she's gonna bring ten grand with her."

Auntie slapped Tad around the back of his head to quiet him. I smiled at the sight of Auntie regaining her spirit and assured myself that even if we lost the inn, she would be fine now that our family was whole.

Pressing my forehead into the warm glass, I looked at every shop we passed. Gyms, tanning salons, supermarkets, box stores, and banks.

Banks.... Banks!

"Fuck! Stop the car!"

"Adam, watch your tongue!"

"Stop where?"

"What's wrong with you, Makani?!"

Tad turned the wheel and pulled into a plaza made up of a small food market, a few restaurants, a hardware store, and the only federal credit union on the island.

They all began pressing me for answers, but I tuned them out as I pulled out my phone, opened a browser, and used my precious data minutes to log into my joint checking account with Jeff, something I had practically ignored for months while I hatched my plan for my clean escape. I didn't want to use it for anything, even emergencies, since he would be able to immediately find me.

But I did remember my username and password. The data indicator spun for well over a minute owing to a weak signal. I held my breath as the page loaded, inch-by-inch, to reveal our multiple accounts until there it was. Joint Checking... $373,023.42.

"Yes!" I dropped my phone and reached over to hug my mother. "Yes, yes, yes!"

"You go crazy, cuz? What's going on!"

"Jeff never took me off our joint checking account with the Credit Union!"

"And?" Tad asked.

"And there's THREE-HUNDRED AND SEVENTY-THREE THOUSAND DOLLARS IN THERE!"

I fished my phone from the seat and waved it in front of Tad's face, leaving him, my mother, and Auntie all dumbstruck, and while they were as shocked as anyone would be, I grabbed my crutches and started hobbling into the bank as quickly as I could.

I only realized once I got inside that I had no clue what I was going to do. Should I withdraw the money? Could I close the account? Cashier's check? I knew I had to speak to a banker but also understood my rights. To direct deposit my paycheck in Atlanta, Jeff added me as a joint holder of the account. That meant I had equal access to the money. In fact, a small chunk of it was already mine. I considered the rest just reimbursement for the bullshit he put me through.

"Sir, can I help you?" an employee asked me, a young woman standing near a podium by the front door. By that time, Auntie and Mom made their way in behind me.

"Yes," I said. "I need to speak with one of the bankers about making some changes to my account."

"Very well. Have a seat. Somebody will be right with you."

I found I didn't even need to sit down. Very quickly, a man met us by the seating area and called us into his private office. Spread out on the table was the morning paper. I cringed at the headline, a picture of me from my social media account, and a lousy photo of Jeff taken from his.

"Mr. Frost, thank you for coming in. I'm Harry Miller. What can I do for you?"

"Adam, please." I cleared my throat, nervous that what I was about to do would raise major red flags.

"I'm here today to figure out my options in regards to my joint account with my now deceased..." I cleared my throat. "Joint-account holder."

"Very well. Do you have the account number and a photo ID?"

I unlocked my phone again and squinted to read the account number listed, but it was incomplete.

"Umm... can I give you my social security number and ID?"

"Yes, that will work."

After I gave Harry the requested information, he tapped it out on the keyboard, gasping when he saw the amount. His forehead started glistening. Beads of sweat formed on his browline. "If you'll excuse me, I need to get the bank manager."

Harry power-walked out of the room, leaving Auntie, Mom, and me alone. The two of them appeared just as nervous as I was. Mom tapped her foot incessantly. Auntie pulled out her silver flask, taking a large swig from it, offering it up to me. I could feel my mom's judgmental eyes as I swallowed the potent, sickly sweet rum down.

"Sorry! I'm nervous."

"Your father was a drinker too, you know. You're not turning into him, are you?"

"I actually think I'm turning into your sister. She's been a terrible influence on me. You should have never let me come here."

Auntie playfully slapped my arm, then took the flask away and hid it before Harry and another man came back into the room.

"Hello, Adam. Alana and Luana, it's good to see you again." A much older portly man, obviously also a native-Hawaiian, sat down.

"Haka! You still working here? I thought you died years ago!" Auntie perked up at the sight of the old man, then hiccuped, her cheeks already turning flushed from the rum.

"Well, I see you're just as charming as ever." He winked at her, then turned his attention to a paper he set on the desk.

"My employee has told me about your request. And, well, considering what's in the papers and how respected your family is in the community, there's no reason why we can't assign full ownership of the account over to you. So long as you're willing to sign this paperwork confirming the death of Mr. Thatcher?"

He turned the paper around for me to sign. I didn't read much of it. The first few lines summarized that I was stating the truth, which I was. But as I went to sign, my fingers trembled at the thought of such a vast sum of money, an amount I couldn't dream of making in a decade or more.

A few minutes later, we were all back in the car with a slip showing me my account number, a temporary checkbook, and the promise that I would soon receive a checkbook and debit card in the mail.

The four of us sat there in silence, completely unable to process what had happened. No one in my family had ever had access to that much money at once.

It took an hour more to get home, after a quick stop at the tax office to pay Auntie's balance in full. Auntie also insisted we stop in the business registrar's office and add my name to the business registration, making me part-owner in the Estate Inn.

After that, we were both somber and cheerful. I thought about what we had gone through, what losses we had suffered. I was also conflicted because of how happy I was after saving our home.

I thought about the Wright family and wondered what they were doing now. None of this had been easy on them. They were kind people. They didn't deserve any of this.

Our attitude changed when we drove into the parking lot to the sight of my father's white van parked in the same spot as always, halfway between the end of the lot and the door. My asshole of a father leaned against the van, dressed in a suit that made him seem worthy when I knew he was absolutely worthless.

Tad stopped the car near the front door.

"Go inside," I said to Auntie and my mom. "I'll take care of him."

I hopped out of the car and did my best to crutch my way over the deteriorating parking lot, a great deal of it washed away by the hurricane. This left potholes and chunks of concrete scattered everywhere.

My dad immediately noticed my mother. He was obviously unaware that she was on the island and called out to her as she made her way inside, Tad remaining on the porch with his arms folded like an angry, good bodyguard.

"Come on, Luana, don't be like that!" he yelled across the lot. "Come out and say hello!"

The way he spoke to her infuriated me. He sounded just like Jeff. At the same time, he wasn't Jeff. If anything, I could be glad that he left us alone. The only redeeming quality he had in my eyes was that he never laid a hand on us.

"I've told you before, Dad, get off our property, or we'll call the police! You're not welcome here."

He didn't even stop to consider the fact I was on crutches. He showed zero concern whatsoever, despite obviously knowing what had happened considering the rolled-up newspaper sticking out of his back pocket.

"You're kidding me. I just came here to offer your aunt one more chance to sell. Otherwise, it'll be my property to demolish as I see fit."

"That's what you think," I said as I pulled out the tax receipt and handed it to him. He hesitated, but took and read the paper. As he did, all color left his face. He clenched his jaw and crumbled the paper in his fist before tossing it to the ground.

"No, no, no. It's not possible! How the hell did you come up with the money to pay this off! I worked too hard to lose this property. Alana, Luana, come out! Let's talk this over!"

My dad tried to push by me, but after my encounter with Jeff, I knew I was strong enough to fight back. Despite the throbbing in my leg, I balanced on both feet and pushed him back with as much might as I could muster until he was pressed into the van. He certainly wasn't Jeff. He was much older, much weaker, and much, much lighter.

"You don't even care, do you? That Mom almost had to bury her son? That I got shot. That my boyfriend—"

I choked back the words. Flashing back to what happened on Haleakala was still too raw for me.

"Get off our property before I do something I'll regret."

My father, fists still curled, did not back down. He tried to push past me again. I didn't know what he was expecting. Even if he had managed to get by me, he would have had Tad to deal with, not to mention a pissed off Auntie with a cane and my mother with a pocketbook so heavy I thought she kept bricks in there.

It was over in a flash. My father was on the ground, gripping his groin and dry heaving after I whacked him between his legs with my crutch with all my might.

"Way to go, cuz!" Tad cheered from the porch. "Hit him again!"

So I did, sort of. I pushed the bottom of one of my crutches into his shoulder with just enough force to cause him to topple over. Not because I wanted to hurt him again, but because I wanted him rolling around in the dirt in his new, shiny suit. I wanted him to go back to wherever he came from covered in mud and explain to his boss and his boss' boss how he failed his months-long attempt to secure them a multi-million dollar property. Most of all, though, I just wanted him to feel, for one moment, inferior to the family he abandoned.

"Now, before I call Tad over here, I'm going to tell you this one more time, as a new owner of the Estate Inn: Get. The. Fuck. Off. My. Property."

My father scrambled like a pathetic man-child to the driver's seat of his van. I fake-jabbed at him with my crutch. Once he got in, he cursed under his breath, turned the car on, and sped away.

I said a silent prayer to myself that it would be the last encounter with my father for the rest of my life. For my sake, and for my mother and sister, I hoped I was right. I also hoped my jab to his nuts rendered him impotent, so he couldn't inflict his failure on any more children.

I smiled at my mother standing in the doorway, her hand over her heart and her eyes full of pride and love and joy. I knew I didn't need my dad. She was already more than enough parent for me. When Maria arrived, my whole world would once again be on Maui where it belonged.

After days in the hospital, I didn't want to go inside. Instead, I hopped around the side of the house toward the beach. Kicking my shoes and socks off, I carefully stepped across the sand, putting as much weight on my splinted leg as I could. The doctors and nurses instructed me to use my leg more and more every day.

One step after another, my bare feet dug into the white sand until I reached the waterline, and let the warm ocean waves wash over them.

I half expected to feel more messed up than I was, but now, in my paradise sanctuary that was the Estate Inn, I had everything I needed to thrive.

I felt the sand shift. A gentle hand landed on my shoulder and, as the next wave washed over my ankles, two feet filled the void behind me, then to my left side. I finally saw the face I had been waiting to see since I woke up in the hospital. By the time I was walking again, Calder had already been discharged, only he had been airlifted to an orthopedic surgeon on O'ahu at his father's request. I had to wait until he got back to Maui.

"We're quite the mess, aren't we?" he said with one arm in a sling, sporting quite a bruise on his forehead.

I laughed and wanted to hug him desperately, to show him the newfound strength and confidence I had discovered. I was no longer the timid, frail young man he met a few weeks ago. But with my leg and his shoulder, he was right. We were quite a mess.

Tossing one crutch aside, I wrapped my arm around his for support, leaned into him, and stood there, silent, watching the sunset. As the last sliver of golden light slipped over the horizon, I held my breath and silently thanked Princess Popoalaea for giving me my spirit back. She helped me find myself. And she helped me save the man I now realized I truly loved.

As the sky blazed alive with oranges and yellows and reds and blues, Calder tilted his head and kissed me.

"I love you," he said, hesitating as though he had never uttered the words before.

"I love you, too."

He chuckled, sighing out the tension of a moment that I felt went perfectly. Bending down, he kissed me again. Everything felt right. He smiled through his kiss, and when he pulled away, I recognized his dimples for the first time, and I found myself hoping for a lifetime with this fierce, kind, and tender man.

I didn't know where we were headed. We hadn't even been on a first date. I was directionless in love, and that was fine by me.

THE END

ABOUT THE AUTHOR

RJ Castiglione has been creating fantasy and contemporary stories since 2017 when he first released book one of the Fjorgyn LitRPG series. Since then, he has expanded his releases to include Steamtown Chronicles, a Gamelit novella serial, and has been published in Scout Media's "Of Words" anthology with the inclusion of "The Jonathan of Bracken Manor."

In 2016, RJ and his husband relocated from Boston to Rhode Island, where he works from home managing RJ Castiglione Books, traveling across the state of Rhode Island to meet with and sign paperback copies for his most appreciated readers, and writing stories for his readers to enjoy.

RJ is an avid reader and gamer, but he most enjoys traveling with his husband to various destinations around the world to seek inspiration for future stories.

f facebook.com/rjcastiglione
twitter.com/rjcasta
a amazon.com/author/rjcastiglione
g goodreads.com/rjcastiglione

ONE LAST THING

If you enjoyed this book, I'd be very grateful if you'd post a short review on Amazon or Goodreads. Your feedback really does make a difference. I read all the reviews personally so I can make my books even better.

Thanks again for your support!